MW01035193

Peirene

NORA IKSTENA

TRANSLATED FROM THE
LATVIAN BY MARGITA GAILITIS

Mātes Piens

AUTHOR

Nora Ikstena was born in 1969 in Riga, Latvia. She studied at the University of Latvia before moving to New York. On her return to the Baltics she helped establish the Latvian Literature Center. She published her first novel *Celebration of Life* in 1998 and has written over twenty books since. She has won numerous awards such as the Order of the Three Stars for services to literature and the Baltic Assembly Prize. *Soviet Milk*, her most recent novel, won the 2015 Annual Latvian Literature Award (LALIGABA) for Best Prose along with the Dzintars Sodums Prize.

TRANSLATOR

Margita Gailitis has translated some of Latvia's finest poetry and prose into English, including Sandra Kalniete's *With Dance Shoes in Siberian Snows* and Māra Zālīte's *Five Fingers*. *Soviet Milk* is her first translation for Peirene Press.

MEIKE ZIERVOGEL
PEIRENE PRESS

At first glance this novel
depicts a troubled mother–
daughter relationship set
in the Soviet-ruled Baltics
between 1969 and 1989. Yet
just beneath the surface
lies something far more
positive: the story of three
generations of women,
and the importance of a
grandmother in giving
her granddaughter what
her daughter is unable
to provide – love, and
the desire for life.

First published in Great Britain in 2018 by
Peirene Press Ltd
17 Cheverton Road
London N19 3BB
www.peirenepress.com

First published under the original Latvian language title *Mātes Piens* by Dienas
Grāmata, Riga
Copyright © Nora Ikstena, 2015

This translation © Margita Gailitis, 2018
Original translation edit: Vija Kostoff
With special thanks to Sophie Lewis, who edited *Soviet Milk* for Peirene.

ISBN 978-1-908670-42-7

Designed by Sacha Davison Lunt
Photographic Images: elenasz / 123RF Stock Photo (pattern)
Magdalena Roeseler / Flickr CC 4.0 (main image)
Typeset by Tetragon, London
Printed and bound by T J International, Padstow, Cornwall

Supported by

Latvia
100

Latvijas Rakstnieku savienība

Ministry of Culture of the Republic of Latvia

Peirene

NORA IKSTENA

TRANSLATED FROM THE
LATVIAN BY MARGITA GAILITIS

Soviet Milk

1) school milk
   but also
2) the bitter mother's milk

5 yrs OLD

I don't remember 15 October 1969. There are people who swear they remember their birth. I don't. It's likely that I was well positioned in my mother's womb, because the birth was normal. Not particularly long, or particularly short, with the last contractions coming every five minutes. My mother was twenty-five, young and healthy. Her mental state, though, was not so healthy, as I learned later.

I do remember, or at least I can picture, the golden, tender calm of October, alternating with forebodings of a long period of darkness. It's a kind of boundary month, at least in the climate of this latitude, where seasons change slowly and autumn only gradually gives way to winter.

Probably leaves were falling, and our bad-tempered concierge raked them up in the courtyard. She had come from Kyrgyzstan with her family and been allocated a flat in our building at 20 Mičurina Street. Her slant-eyed little girl sat on the windowsill, slurping borscht and cheerfully inviting everyone into their home. The pre-war grandeur of the flat had been modified to reflect the Kyrgyz woman's idea of beauty. The previous inhabitants, a Jewish family, had abandoned the flat in 1941, when deportation to Siberia saved them from having to wear yellow stars on their backs a few months later, in Nazi-occupied Riga. Now heavy rugs covered the parquet, the porcelain dishes were filled with sunflower seeds and spittoons stood on the piano lid. Times and religions had commingled. And that's how it was in the entire building, when I was carried up to the thirteenth flat, carefully swaddled like a chrysalis, as was the custom in those times.

Now and then I have a dream from which I awake feeling sick. I'm clinging to my mother's breast and trying to suck on it. The breast is large, full of milk, but I can't get any out. I don't see my mother, she doesn't help me, and I'm left to struggle with her breast on my own. Then suddenly I succeed and a bitter, repulsive liquid spurts into my mouth. I gag and wake with a start.

My mother was a young doctor. Perhaps she knew that her milk would have caused more harm than good to her child. How else to explain her disappearance from home immediately after giving birth? She was missing for five days. She returned with aching breasts. Her milk had stopped flowing.

In despair, my grandmother fed me camomile tea for two days. Then she went to the infant clinic. The suspicious doctor berated her in Russian and insulted my mother for abandoning me. But eventually he wrote out a note authorizing her to receive infant formula for me.

During the twenty years I lived with my mother, I wasn't able to ask her why she had deprived me of her breast. I wasn't able to because I didn't yet know that she had. And it would have been an inappropriate question because, as it turned out, the role of mother was to become mine.

*   _her mother's birthday_
        19 yrs old

I don't remember 22 October 1944, but I can reconstruct it. Riga has been liberated from the Nazis. Bombs have shattered the maternity ward's windows. It is damp and cold, and the women who have just given birth helplessly wrap themselves in their bloodied sheets. Exhausted nurses and doctors are bundling up dead newborns and drinking as they work. An epidemic that everyone is calling nasal typhoid fever is raging through the hospital. Sounds of wailing, bombs whistling in the air and, through the windows, the smell of burning. My mother has sneaked me out of the ward, bound to her chest, and is squirting her milk into my nose. Pus, milk and blood together drip from my tiny nose. I gag and breathe, gag and breathe.

Then there is silence. A horse pulls a wagon on a sunny autumnal road from Riga to Babīte in the outskirts. My father stops several times to allow my mother to feed me. I no longer gag but breathe calmly and greedily suck my mother's milk. In the Babīte Forest district we have a lovely house, barely furnished and without a cradle, but my mother makes up a bed for me in a suitcase.

Each morning my father inspects his young spruce trees. That's what happens until Christmas, when a heavy lorry full of soldiers roars in. They shout in a language my parents don't understand, then jump out and begin to fell the young spruce trees. My father locks my mother and me in the back room, where she hides me in the suitcase with holes pierced in it so I can breathe. My father runs out of the house, yelling, 'Bastards, scoundrels!' and trying to save his spruce trees. The soldiers beat him until he bleeds and throw him into the lorry with the hewn trees. Then they search the house, banging at all the doors. Holding her breath, my mother crouches in a wardrobe in the locked room, holding the suitcase with me inside it on her knees. The soldiers are ransacking the house, the noise is horrendous. Finally, all grows quiet and we listen to the sound of the engine as they drive away.

Towards morning my mother climbs out of the wardrobe. She feeds me, ties me to herself, dresses warmly and heads back to Riga on foot. It is late evening when we arrive at our flat on Tomsona Street, soon to be renamed Mičurina Street. My mother is exhausted but she still has to tape over the windows shattered by bombs during an air raid. Otherwise we would both freeze.

*

I don't know how my mother and grandmother dealt with my mother's disappearance at the time, but it was never mentioned. Throughout my childhood the smell of medicine and disinfectant replaced the fragrance of mother's milk. These chemicals would hang like a cloud around my mother: there when she returned from exhausting night duty at the maternity hospital; still there when, after long hours of wakefulness, she caught up on sleep at home. Her handbag was full of pills, ampoules and various steel instruments. Later I recognized them as terrifying gynaecologists' instruments. It was a macabre world. If my mother happened to be home at night, she would sit up smoking and drinking coffee, bent over mountains of lamplit medical books. Pinned above her desk were diagrams of wombs, ovaries, pelvises and vaginas from various angles and perspectives.

My mother knew nothing of the world beyond. She would pointedly close her door when the programme *Vremya* – 'Time' – came on television, with lisping Leonid Ilyich Brezhnev. She didn't read the *Riga's Voice* newspaper, for which a long queue formed on the corner of Gorky Street every evening. The lunchtime queue at the meat and dairy shop was equally long. You could buy the popular so-called doctor's sausage and butter there – but she had no idea of this domestic world. Yet beside the mountains of medical textbooks lay a half-read *Moby-Dick*. It spoke of her longing for a life of the mind that remained beyond her grasp.

I don't remember Mother ever hugging me much, but I remember her needle-pricked thigh, where she practised injections. I remember her in bed with blue lips the first time she overdosed, possibly as part of some medical experiment. I remember the smell of her dressing gown, the odour of the bitter tincture given before she was driven to the hospital. And I remember the corridor of the maternity hospital where I was allowed to meet her after night shifts. We would then head for an Aloja Street café and eat *solyanka* soup and *kupati* sausages, and she would add caffeine from an ampoule to her coffee. I also remember how our street seemed frozen in time, like a picture clipped from a different era and glued into today. Only the elegant types frequenting the races at the nearby hippodrome were missing. In their place, going home or to work, heads bowed, other kinds of people were hurrying towards Communism, their net bags filled with humble supplies: long loaves, bottles of kefir milk with bright green screw tops, laundry parcels wrapped in grey paper and tied with string.

*

At least nine years had passed since the felling of the young spruce trees. I was one of the best students so I was given a part in the school's devised montage for assembly. I had to hold a very large letter 'M', and together with my classmates we formed the statement: '*Mi za mir!*' – 'We're for peace!' Each morning a clean, freshly ironed apron lay ready for me, and my mother would do my hair so that it either hung in plaits down my back or was looped up and pinned behind my ears. She cherished me. One day a tall, kind-looking man appeared in our flat. My mother said, 'This is your stepfather.' When he left that evening, I saw my mother crying for the first time. She was sitting in our long, narrow kitchen, which looked out onto the courtyard, a simmering pan full of pumpkin scenting the air from the wood stove.

She looked up and said, 'Your dear papa was taken away because he tried to save his dear spruce trees. Did he have to do that? Had he not run out, had he not tried to stop them, he would still be with us. But he loved the forest and his spruce trees, and he did run out. He was beaten up and taken away. I looked for him for three days. I found him at Šķirotava station, locked up in the carriage that would take him to Siberia. Disfigured by his wounds and very weak, he reached through the bars and gripped me tightly, until a guard saw us and whacked his hand with a rifle butt, catching mine in a glancing blow at the same time. I heard no more from your papa after that. Not a word, not a sign. Until someone from far away brought the news that he had died. That was five years ago. Dead, dear child, your dear papa.'

I don't remember sadness. I remember my mother's tearful voice, every word spoken with such tenderness: dear child, dear papa, dear spruce trees. I liked my handsome stepfather. I didn't – I couldn't – remember my father.

Then one afternoon at the kiosk not far from school – the one with the automat selling carbonated water, which I was categorically forbidden to buy, though it was what I most longed for – a tall, portly man appeared and said he was my father. I burst into tears and ran home as fast as my legs would carry me. There I found my mother as white as a sheet. He was not dead: he had returned.

granddaughter
(in her own voice)

*

I don't remember any occasions when my mother took me
to school or waited to pick me up after lessons. This was
always done by my step-grandfather, who had adopted
her. We used to walk along Gorky Street, a tribute to
the legendary Russian writer, refreshed by the fragrance
of hops floating over from Barbusse Street, which was
named for a French writer. These brief walks spoke to
me of peace and home.

I wasn't afraid of Uncle Sam, or of nuclear war; I
was afraid of my mother. Sometimes a demonic force
seemed to possess her, compelling her to destroy everything around her, especially the love of those she held
dearest. At these times she hated her mother, hated her
stepfather even more, and hated the fact of her own
birth. She would lock herself in the bathroom and howl,
while I stood paralysed at the far end of the corridor, her
howls shuddering through my young bones, her suffering infinite and incomprehensible, a railing against the
injustice of fate, against the inexplicable wreck of a life.

Those moments of great darkness were relieved by
occasional rays of light. We would sit in the living room
with the windows open. Savoury cooking smells and children's voices at play would come drifting in. My mother
would be drawing with coloured pencils on a large sheet of
paper: a depiction of a birth. I was sitting in her lap, and I
wasn't afraid. First she drew a smiling baby in a mother's
tummy, then she drew the baby's head peering out between

the mother's legs – the grimace on the baby's face reflected the suffering and horror awaiting her out here. Then she drew the mother and baby joined only by their umbilical cord, and the scissors that would cut the cord. And then she drew the mother with the infant in her arms, gazing at her with tender, frightened eyes. I followed my mother's pencil strokes. Her hand was small and white with broken nails, her palms dry and cracked from constant washing and the talcum powder which had to be shaken into her rubber gloves. I sat in my mother's lap; I wasn't afraid. I leaned over and pressed my cheek against her hand.

*

Grandmother (in daughter's voice)

My mother resolved to have no regrets. She married my stepfather, who adopted me and loved me like his own daughter. We never talked about my real father. My mother also never learned about my visits to my father, which continued for many years. Already gravely ill on his return from deportation, he lived in a communal flat in what had previously been the pantry. It was permanently damp and the floor was covered with newspapers. He was always drunk.

In his more sober moments, he would recall his years as a student at the University of Latvia, his research into forest plantations and his aversion to fraternities. He remembered his own mother used to dress him up as a young nobleman and call him Zhano. 'You, my daughter, have blue blood,' he would claim, for his father was not the Dobele town shoemaker whom his mother had married but a German baron. My father was one of the silent legion who could never adjust to Soviet reality. He did not live to see the deaths of Brezhnev and Andropov, nor the advent of Gorbachev or the Baltic Way to freedom.

Having witnessed my father's physical suffering, I decided to become a doctor. I'm not sure I loved him. Sometimes I felt sorry for him. Sometimes I hated him because I suspected that his self-destructive gene was deeply implanted in me and that with time it would grow and strengthen, no matter how hard I fought it.

I remember the day my father died very well. Another tenant answered the door: the warm-hearted Jewish woman, who had often treated me to sticky glazed pretzels. Sobbing, she held me close against her soft, crocheted shawl. Then she led me to my father's room.

There he was – emaciated, gaping. Two days after his death, the others in the flat had broken through his door.

Beneath him, on the stained day bed and all over the floor, newspapers displayed the faces of smiling workers and stern Politburo members. He was lying among words that promised five-year growth in a single year and extolled the superior morality of the people who were building Communism. It was they who had demanded the construction of new cities in distant Siberia, where thousands of innocents were sent to die without learning the nature of their crimes. He was lying among words advocating the diversion of rivers, the conversion of churches into storehouses for mineral fertilizers, and the destruction of the literature, art and sculpture of our Latvian heritage.

Thus he lay: one of the many who had surrendered quietly, dying in an obscure corner because he could not adjust and swallow humiliation, shame, dishonour and disillusionment. Discarded on the waste heap of our times. Most likely he was buried in a common grave for the homeless on the outskirts of the city. My mother showed no interest in him and never learned of his death. She protected her new life and in doing so did her best to protect me.

grand daughter

*

My grandmother and step-grandfather were the closest thing I had to parents. My mother stood somewhere outside the family. Our lives revolved around her; we depended on her – but not for maternal nurturing. Now and then, her struggles with her demons and angels would spill over into our daily routine, forcing us to acknowledge the fragile boundary between life and death. Worried, we would stay up, waiting for her to return home. And every time she came in we would sigh with relief, despite not knowing what the next day or night would bring. Not one of us knew much about my father. My grandmother thought it likely that they'd met at a country dance, which she had forced my mother to attend. Her pregnancy had come after that. This was all we knew. But I fantasized about that meeting.

Preparing an instant coffee in her aunt's small kitchen, my mother hears a reminder on the crackly battery-powered radio that it's January 1969. One of those youthful January mornings when she would hurry to finish memorizing the idiocies of science under Communism, and devote the rest of her time to questions of medicine and the origins of life, and to reading photocopies of smuggled books by Pasternak and Sartre. She would be a doctor and a scientist, come what may. For the moment she easily manages to regurgitate the official programme, while simultaneously acquiring a totally different, prohibited education. Her mother and aunt are worried about her. My mother can spend days in her room, just reading books. She's already nearly twenty-five, but has never been seen with a young man. Is she attractive? She has delicate bones, small hands and firm round breasts, light hair which she occasionally bleaches, and freckles. She's not concerned about what she wears. She even goes to university in wide, comfortable trousers, although she can feel the shocked stares of her instructors and fellow students. Trousers are only acceptable on Saturdays or when working at the *kolkhoz*. At all other times one has to wear skirts reaching to mid-knee or, of course, conservative minis, when they're in fashion.

While her aunt fries potatoes for her husband's breakfast, my mother drinks bitter coffee, gazes out of the window and thinks about the great whale with which the captain is obsessed in *Moby-Dick*.

In the evening her mother and aunt make her put on a dress that their brother has sent from England. She must go to the village dance and stop burrowing among those books. The local band will be playing, there will be refreshments and, crucially, dancing. May the city bookworm dance up a storm with the country boys. The two sisters drive her right to the door.

What she sees inside doesn't compare to anything she's experienced before. On the stage a singer is gesturing stiffly. Several couples are moving around the dance floor, some freestyle, others waltzing. At the side of the room hefty country girls with self-fashioned beehives crowd around the buffet tables. Young men fidget on the other side.

What is she doing here? She doesn't understand; it is a kind of *bitiye* and *nichto* – a Sartrean being and nothingness. But the English dress soon attracts stares. As does her smooth, blonde boy's haircut.

She hopes that her mother and aunt are no longer standing at the door like the mythical Cerberus, ready to push her back through the seven circles of hell. To make sure, she'll stay a little while longer. Then she'll leave, will sit by the lake and afterwards go home, as if she had danced her fill and the young man who accompanied her home had been too shy to come in.

She settles in a corner and, gazing at the dancing couples, almost cheers up. Then a young man saunters towards her across the dance floor. She hopes he'll change direction but soon it's clear: he's coming straight for her.

Politely, he asks her to dance. She doesn't even remember that she could say no. She simply gives him her hand and they join the dancers. He waltzes with assurance. Now and then his cheek touches hers and she realizes that this isn't unpleasant. Between dances they do as the other couples: stand apart, not knowing what to do with their hands, waiting for the next song to begin. After the tenth dance he suggests they have some wine. There's a crowd at the tables but he easily slips through the crush and surfaces with two full glasses. They sit down at the side of the room.

She's going to be a doctor, a scientist.

He is working in a mechanics workshop for the time being. How did she happen to be here?

She's staying with her mother's sister at the farm.

How does she like it in the countryside?

Fine. If she had her books, she could live in the country.

How does she plan to earn money?

She'll be a scientist.

Ah. He'd like to study to be an aviation engineer. Would she like to dance some more?

No.

Can he accompany her home?

Yes.

The January night is unusually warm. They walk down to the lake, which is still not iced over. He gathers some flat stones and shows her how to make them skip. Just as her thoughts skip over the surface when she tries to understand Feuerbach. The stone brushes the water's surface and then flies up again, but to earn her diploma she'll have to explain Feuerbach's atheism – the stone sinks.

He invites her to drink some tea with him, in a nearby guard's hut, where they spend the night.

*

After my father's death I slowly grew to hate both my mother and our general situation. Troubled by her own history, she urged me to learn everything my teachers wanted, not to talk back and to be an active member of the Communist youth organizations. My mother was protected by my stepfather. Once a soldier in the victorious army of the Great Patriotic War, both his service in the guard of Latvia's president and his brother's voluntary enlisting in the German army were obscured by this illustrious background. The bloody polka of history.

My mother and stepfather would discuss their brothers late into the night. My stepfather's brother had been executed as a traitor, before which he'd been tortured for some previous, unspecified betrayal. 'Those Russian dogs,' my stepfather would mutter. I didn't understand. He had marched shoulder to shoulder with those dogs almost as far as Berlin, and enjoyed May and November festivities with them, and received a food parcel with rarities such as dry-cured sausage, instant coffee and marinated pickles and tomatoes.

My mother's brother was alive and well in London. He owned a cloth factory and sent packages with things unseen here: beautiful fabrics, skeins of wool and patterns, from which my mother sewed our clothes. Twice a year my mother sent the Soviet agencies a request for permission to visit him. Twice a year she received an official reply with the decision *netselesoobrazno* – nonessential. Her ten-year communication with the regime ended once again with *netselesoobrazno*: the response to her last request for permission to go to London, for her brother's funeral.

Despite these absurdities, my mother continued to raise me as an honourable and faithful young Soviet citizen. Yet within me blossomed a hatred for the duplicity and hypocrisy of this existence. We carried flags in the May and November parades in honour of the Red Army, the Revolution and Communism, while at home we crossed ourselves and waited for the English army to come and free Latvia from the Russian boot.

Having honourably fulfilled my hypocritical role at school, I grew bookish and withdrawn. When a professor living on the floor above us died, the new tenants simply jettisoned his library via the window. An enormous heap of books built up in the yard. My mother didn't hide her disapproval when I lugged the old multi-volume medical encyclopedia up the stairs, but she didn't object, so as not to widen the breach between us.

And here it all was: the truth about the wretched, hypocritical creature we call man. A muddle of blood vessels, convolutions of intestines, glands and secretions, lymph nodes and arteries, phalli and vaginas, testicles and wombs. In this narrative, death was just an accidental, unavoidable stopping point.

*

Thinking about my mother, about her birth and mine, I can't help thinking about predetermination, or maybe some great, incomprehensible plan. I picture my mother not as a medical student in Soviet Latvia carrying an unwanted baby in the grey Riga autumn but instead with a bandanna tied around her forehead, her fat tummy half-bared, in that parallel world where freedom reigns and The Who are singing at Woodstock.

In spite of the historical impossibility, there was something of the flower child in my mother. She wasn't afraid of experimenting with herself and spent periods in a haze – whether through the use of some substance or thanks to her refusal to countenance the place and time in which she was fated to be alive. I remember her once, drunk on wine and high in a field of dandelions by the hippodrome, where the horses no longer raced. For her the hippodrome was evidence of some other, carefree and unfettered life. She ran through the dandelions like a young mare, and I skipped alongside getting under her feet. Out of breath, she lay down among the dandelions and I flopped down with her. There we lay, and the world had no limits.

*

I achieved my dream: the Riga Medical Institute accepted me. Officials there clung to the pre-war tradition by which doctors all came from Jewish families. Newcomers found it hard to break in. But I was difficult to stop.

On the kitchen table stood an unknown departed's skull, which my stepfather had dug up in an abandoned country graveyard and steeped in various liquids until it had achieved a bluish-white sheen. Morning and night, eye to eye with the skull, I recited my Lord's Prayer of bones in Latvian and Latin: *Spārnkauls – os sphenoidale, pakauša kauls – os occipitale, deniņu kauls – os temporale, paura kauls – os parietale, pieres kauls – os frontale, sietiņkauls – os ethmoidale, augšžokļa kauls – maxilla, vaiga kauls – os zygomaticum, aukslēju kauls – os palatinum, asaru kauls – os lacrimale, deguna kauls – os nasale, mēles kauls – os hyoideum...*

My best friend was the anatomy lab's Cadaver Mārtiņš, as he was known. For a measure of vodka he would let you into the locked rooms at night. He would fish the required body part out of the formalin tank for me. I could spend hours dissecting, preparing and sewing it up. To solve life's puzzle you had to use death's rebus as a guide.

An old professor noticed my diligence. He said that I had an unusual drive to unlock the body's secrets for a young woman. Also that my mind was too clever and wouldn't do me any good in the long run. He said I must learn to accept that the key to life or death did not lie in my hands. He insisted that there is something more than existence, something we may not mention. The old man had nothing to lose. One evening, finding me bent over a uterus in formalin, he asked, 'Do you believe in God?' This was hard to answer, given that all references to anything divine had been erased from printed materials under the Soviet regime.

'I still haven't had the opportunity to meet Him,' I said.

*

I was seven or eight years old when I temporarily became nearly mute. It was a lovely autumn afternoon. A friend and I were collecting the leaves that were beginning to turn yellow around the hippodrome. From over the trees, the smell of burning grew pervasive. It didn't seem suspicious because people often used to burn things in their gardens in the autumn.

But the smell became stronger and suddenly, through the hippodrome roof, enormous flames shot out. They leapt along the beautiful building with unbelievable speed, and soon human yells as well as ambulance and fire engine sirens could be heard. We stood as if turned to stone, gazing at this disastrous scene, our pockets full of leaves. My mother flew from one of the ambulances. Screaming, she rushed to the firemen, grabbed a pail, scooped up water from a marshy ditch and raced in the direction of the fire-riddled building. Crying miserably, I ran to be with her. The firefighters caught up with us among the stands in the main arena, just as the burning roof collapsed.

In the ambulance, they injected my mother with something to calm her. Stuttering, I struggled to say only one word. I remember that short journey from the burning hippodrome to our building so well. I led my mother by the hand. Staring blankly, she obediently came along with me. I continued to cry and to stammer that one word: 'home'.

It was a real Walpurgis Night. The calming effect of the injection soon wore off and my mother spent the night demolishing her room. My grandmother locked me in the bathroom, while my step-grandfather tried to get into my mother's room. 'Butchers,' she screamed, 'butchers, butchers, butchers!' My grandmother stood weeping at the glass door, pleading for her to be quiet. Then my mother began a long, wailing cry. Soon, worried neighbours were knocking on our door. Then all went silent. A silence that blended into the darkness of the bathroom, where I sat sobbing and still trying quietly to say the word 'home'.

*

It was a lovely summer's day in 1977. In the morning after night duty, the head doctor called me in. He said an opportunity had arisen to supplement my education in gynaecology and endocrinology in Leningrad. After the abattoir – as we called night duty in our jargon – with its ever-spinning wheel of births, caesarean sections, scheduled legal and spontaneous abortions, myomas, polyps and cysts – to go to Leningrad and concentrate on science seemed incredible. I had to go to Engels Street to apply and submit to a short interview. It was just a formality.

I was tempted by this antechamber of hell on Engels Street. Maybe I would be let into paradise; maybe I would have to pay for it in blood. I fortified myself with coffee and a caffeine ampoule. I headed past our building, where my stepfather was preparing breakfast while my mother braided my daughter's hair for school. Past their life, where I didn't fit, but inhabited it like a ghost from another world to whose mystery I was increasingly drawn.

Just a formality, the head doctor had said. I was going to the building in whose cellars four years before my birth, just as a formality, the newly formed Soviet regime in Latvia had slaughtered innocent people, and their blood had coursed away through specially constructed gutters to mingle with Riga's waste water. The prisoners crowded into tiny airless rooms with naked bulbs overhead had waited either for death or to be deported to Siberia. Such were those times. Crimes against the regime were an everyday occurrence. I had to go through the formality of this circle of hell. Leningrad was waiting for me with its new scientific discoveries and free spirit, which oppressed Riga was not allowed.

Inside the Engels Street building an elegant gentleman in civilian clothes led me to his office.

'You're a very talented young doctor, but you have a complicated background. Make your replies to my questions brief and clear. Did you ever meet your father?'

'No.'

'Did you know he was a traitor to his country?'

'No.'

'If you had known, would you have contacted him?'

'No.'

'Did your mother ever talk to you about your brother?'

'No.'

'Did you know that he was engaged in spreading anti-Soviet propaganda in London?'

'No.'

'Did you ever want to meet him?'

'No.'

'What exactly did you mean by these words, which were said on — at — o'clock in the anatomy laboratory: "I still haven't had the opportunity to meet him"? Who is this he?'

'God.'

'Do you believe in God?'

'No.'

'Thank you. We will notify your head doctor of our decision regarding your studies in Leningrad.'

In the afternoon the head doctor phoned to congratulate me on being given the opportunity to supplement my education in Leningrad. An hour later we had to

rush to the hippodrome, which was consumed in blue
flames. I managed to throw all sorts of ampoules into my
bag. I was furious and determined to save the people. I
know they injected me with a sedative. I don't remember
any more.

daughter (granddaughter

*

When my mother returned from Leningrad, suddenly
she no longer had work. She was withdrawn. She only
emerged to make coffee or tea. Our lives went on in
two parallel worlds. In our room the morning started
early. My step-grandfather prepared breakfast, my grandmother ironed my school uniform and braided my hair. I
organized my school books, notebooks, pencil case and
pencils, fountain pen and rubber. Then my grandmother
accompanied me to school, holding my hand all the way.

I studied hard but always counted the hours until
school was over and my step-grandfather would be waiting for me outside. He was noticeably older than the
other parents, but he was always handsomely dressed
and distinguished-looking, being so tall. Walking home
from school, we often lingered about the queues at the
meat and dairy shops, in the hope of picking something
up there, 'thrown out' as if to animals, as we used to say
in those lean years. Afterwards we would stop again,
to queue at the kiosk for the evening newspaper. Only
then would we go home to sausages with potatoes and
sauerkraut.

In the evenings the television would be on. It informed us in Russian and Latvian about the thriving country in which we lived. My grandmother hung on every word of our great leader Leonid Ilyich Brezhnev's long speeches. She was convinced that Brezhnev had ill-fitting dentures. She claimed to be afraid that they might fall out of his mouth.

Occasionally on these evenings I went to see my mother in her room. It was filled with books, piles of papers, dirty cups and ashtrays overflowing with cigarette butts. Apathetic and bored, my mother would be sitting on her bed, flipping through notes. She paid little attention to her visitor from next door. I would sit for a while, looking at her and her room, then quietly leave.

I remember the afternoon when, instead of my step-grandfather, I found my mother waiting for me. She kissed me, took my school bag and told me that we were going to the market. We almost never shopped in the market because everything there was expensive. Dark-skinned men displayed large suitcases full of wonders: fragrant yellow melons, avocados, bunches of white grapes and orange fruits which they called *hurma* – persimmons. My mother allowed me to choose whatever I desired. I chose two avocados, a persimmon and a handful of some nuts – my mother said these were edible chestnuts and I thought this incredible.

This market day was so different from our usual days. After buying our foreign fruit, my mother sat me down at a table in the market café. She ordered hot chocolate for two and asked me if I would like to go to the country with her. She had been offered a job at a small ambulatory health-care centre. It would be good for us both – to have a little house of our own, a garden and possibly a cat or a dog. I sat holding my bag of fruit and with childish rapture tried to envisage this brand-new, lovely life. But what about my grandparents?

'You'll come to visit them as often as you wish,' my mother said.

Walking back, the nearer we came to our home, the more impossible this opportunity seemed. In the kitchen I saw them both, visibly devastated. Obviously my mother had already talked to them. She left the three of us alone. We hugged each other and cried. It couldn't be helped.

*

While I was supplementing my studies in Leningrad, I stayed at Larisa Nikolayevna's old-fashioned flat on Neva Prospect. The old woman turned my fantasy world into reality. She refused to call St Petersburg Leningrad and remembered not only, as she said, *bylaya roskosh* – the times of former grandeur – but also the time of the city blockade, when people had to eat newspapers and glue. She wasn't interested in medicine, but in the evenings she could talk for hours about Yesenin. She did not consider him a great poet, but the rumours of his disappearance or death interested her. 'Thus many of ours have disappeared,' she would say.

I wasn't interested in conspiracy theories. In the mornings I went to the Institute. There I met up with my Russian female colleagues, who survived on coffee, cigarettes, caffeine ampoules and boiled beetroot. They dressed in thick pullovers and wide trousers, sported boyish haircuts and were obsessed with deciphering the mysteries of fertility and infertility. They conversed in an intelligent Russian, now and then interspersed with robust swear words. In the evenings they drank diluted spirits but by morning they were fresh and attentive, bent over their microscopes.

Exhausted by endless examination of cell samples, in the evenings we sipped our spirits and pondered Brodsky's poetry. He said that life was a pendulum which, once swung to the left, had only to swing back again. Just six years earlier he had been banished from Russia. He was now wandering somewhere on the streets of New York. In Leningrad, we shuffled along on the thin ice of freethinking.

Larisa Nikolayevna's neighbour Serafima was a decent Russian woman who submitted to her husband's abuse. He was a war invalid who drank and beat her. The more he hit his wife, the more she loved him. And she never lost hope of becoming a mother. Every morning and evening she would creep quietly into the pantry, where she had hidden her tiny icons and candles. There Serafima would pray to the Mother of God for a baby. She often came to visit us, always bringing a treat: cabbage-stuffed *pirogi*, *vareniki* dumplings, meat patties or borscht. We would eat in Larisa Nikolayevna's kitchen and Serafima would sing a mournful song about a child who won't come to its mother: '*Miloye ditya, kak zhe ya bez tebya*' – 'How can I be without you, my baby?'

I did not feel the same longing as Serafima. I had carried and given birth to a child, but I had no maternal instincts. Something had excluded me from this mystery, which I wanted to investigate to the very core, to discover its true nature. I disappeared for days so I wouldn't have to feed my child. My milk was bitter: the milk of incomprehension, of extinction. I protected my child from it.

Serafima sang – and in my head an experiment was born. How to circumvent Mother Nature and snub God, whose existence I had denied in hell's antechamber. My women colleagues at the Institute were ready to take part. But I had to convince Serafima.

Late one evening in Larisa Nikolayevna's kitchen I described to Serafima what had to happen but was not happening in her body to create a child. I drew Serafima's ovary and the released ovum, to which rushed a whole army of her boozing and abusing husband's spermatozoa, which turned out to be so feeble that they couldn't occupy Serafima's fortress. She gazed at me with round, frightened eyes, crossed herself several times and repeated, '*Upasi Gospodi. Upasi Gospodi*' – 'God forbid! God forbid!' Then I screwed up my courage and said, 'I'm going to help your bastard of a husband in this struggle, because you want this from the very bottom of your good and pious heart.' Serafima froze. 'No, no, dear

Serafima, it'll be the two of you alone. I'll just extend my doctor's helping hand.'

Serafima thought for three days and three nights, then she made a decision. On her next fertile day, she came to meet us at the Institute. Tucked under her arm to keep it warm, she had brought her abuser's preserved sperm. We warmed it further on our radiators, then introduced it into Serafima's uterus. For half a day she slept in the Institute with her legs raised. Then she went home. After some time it was confirmed that she was expecting a child. She rushed into Larisa Nikolayevna's kitchen and embraced my legs. 'You're a saint, a saint, a true saint!'

daughts/g daughts

*

We could see the silhouette of the old town. Then the new residential districts flashed by, where people lived in identical flats with identical mats at their doors. In the mornings the indistinct mass of them streamed to their workplaces. They streamed back again in the evenings to watch the same unfathomable television broadcasts about their motherland. All this we left behind as the train passed through forests and fields, and the houses and people at the stations grew fewer. Eventually we got out at a small country station. The train disappeared whistling into the distance. Mother lit a cigarette, and our new life began.

For a while my mother and I followed the railway tracks. 'Be careful of the points,' she said. 'Watch that your foot doesn't get caught.' I counted the railway ties as my small feet stepped over each one. In the next few years, those tracks were to become my place of contemplation. They brought me closer to my grandparents, who now lived in expectation of my visits. The freight trains that rushed by often scattered kernels of yellow corn onto the embankment. Picking them out of the gravel, I soothed my longing and shortened the long days and weeks of separation.

For the time being, along with the spring, my mother and I did seem to be beginning a new life. The white and blue anemones greeted us from the ditches. The sky was clear, and somewhere in the distance a cuckoo called. The birches were still in that brilliant, bare greenness that dazzles one's eyes. The spring air mingled with my mother's cigarette smoke and heralded something new. It drove away the sadness of separation.

In our small house at the edge of the village everything was different. Water had to be fetched from the well, the cooking stove and the pot-bellied stove that heated the house used firewood. The waterless toilet gave off an unpleasant smell. But school and my mother's workplace, the ambulatory centre, were less than a ten-minute walk away. And we had an overgrown garden in which yellow forest tulips, a couple of plum trees, a mature cherry tree and a cluster of bushes were all blossoming.

My first school day was dreadful. My mother led me to the old brick building and threw me into the lion's den. The country children were full of suspicion. They stared at me as if I had arrived from a different planet. Their only satisfaction lay in thinking up ways to humiliate me. The teacher looked on with indifference, for she in her turn viewed my mother with great suspicion.

The first month of my new life passed in a fog of tears. Each day after school I walked to the railway tracks, sat on the embankment edge and gazed into the distance. There I allowed my imagination to carry me back to the city and to my grandparents.

My mother left for work early in the morning and returned late at night. I had to take care of myself. I learned how to fire up the wood stove, to bring in water, to do the laundry and to make soup. I lived in one room with a dog which had adopted our home. He was a good and faithful friend, but he passed his fleas on to me.

daughter / mother

*

In Leningrad, Serafima changed in front of our eyes. Every other day she would arrive at the Institute with baked treats. She swore that peace and enlightenment had descended upon her husband. He had almost given up drinking, was polite and attempting to take care of her. She was carrying his child, after all. We female doctors were quite a company. Meddlesome bluestockings only interested in cell cultures, the view through our microscopes, complex theories, coffee, cigarettes, more coffee and alcohol. We screwed up our marriages as badly as we mothered our children. And then there was Serafima: an icon of milk and blood, the faithful wife, the blossoming Madonna, the living experiment to prove all our theories.

Serafima grew attached to me, as one does to a teacher or a saint. I couldn't stand the looks she gave me, combining a childlike naiveté and admiration with something akin to a dog's faithfulness. Often, when no one was looking, she would try to caress me or make the sign of a cross over me. I tried to hide my annoyance, in order not to hurt her.

One afternoon at the Institute when we were sitting with glasses of tea I told Serafima that I had a daughter. Not only was I not a good mother, but I didn't feel like a mother at all. Serafima gazed at me with fearful eyes and told me not to say any more. I kept talking. I wanted to sever the umbilical cord of Serafima's admiration. I told her that I didn't believe in God, and that I didn't want to feed my milk to my daughter, so that she couldn't suck my vileness in with it.

'Vileness?' Serafima exclaimed.

'Yes, Serafima, vileness, this *bes* – the devil, as it's called in your language.'

'But there's no *bes* in you, you're a saint,' Serafima exclaimed, and it issued so naturally from the bottom of her heart that I was stunned.

She took my hand, placed it on her expanding stomach and said, 'You gave me this.' She gazed at me with clear, shining eyes, and for a moment I felt it. A mother's joy, filling this empty, inhospitable corridor with a tender light. It bestowed sense on a senseless era.

That evening I stayed later at the Institute. The conversation with Serafima had stirred a longing for my daughter, a feeling I hadn't had for a good while. I wanted to comb her long, rebellious hair, to braid it properly. With my mind's eye I saw the room where the three of them were having their dinner: my daughter, my mother and my stepfather. My stepfather was surely reading a historical novel about the Stalingrad battle, my mother was knitting or mending something, and my daughter was carefully doing her mathematics or handwriting homework. On the television the news programme had ended and Nora Bumbiere and Viktors Lapčenoks were singing '*Laternu stundā*' – 'In the Lantern Hour'.

I left the Institute at the lantern hour, just as the gaslights were coming on, and hurried to get to the River Neva before they raised the bridges.

Larisa Nikolayevna had become accustomed to my late arrivals home. That night she was waiting for me in the kitchen. She was pale, and on the table before her were a glass of water and a tiny medicine bottle. Serafima had come home with her face badly bruised. Her husband had gone crazy over some trivial thing – drunk, probably. They had had words and he had begun to hit her. Larisa Nikolayevna had helped Serafima wash her face, placed compresses on it and brewed a calming tea. Then Serafima had gone back home. Larisa Nikolayevna had not managed to go to sleep yet.

Something took hold of me. I took the meat-tenderizing mallet and, without removing my coat, went out into the stairwell and over to Serafima's flat. The door was half-open. Serafima's husband sat drinking in the kitchen. She had fallen into a painful sleep in the semi-darkness of the back room. '*O sosedka, prisyad,*' he said – 'Ah, neighbour, have a seat.' We drank a shot each. '*Vydyom pokurim,*' I said – 'Let's go out.' We went out into the stairwell and lit up. '*Khorosho pyotsya,*' he said – 'That was a good drink.' Then I pulled out the meat-tenderizing mallet and hit that bastard in the face several times. And, being drunk, he just howled as if he was being slaughtered.

*

Sometimes after school I would make for my mother's ambulatory centre and wait for her there. They had one long, narrow corridor, always filled with women sitting on benches, tightly packed together. Some of them were pregnant. My mother tried to give each one as much time as she needed. She often finished work late in the evening.

Usually, I would go straight home after school and prepare supper, which my mother would eat later more out of politeness than hunger. Exhausted, she often went to bed without undressing. I would pull off her boots and cover her with a heavy blanket. I would have to wait for the wood to burn down to cinders before I could close the stove door and go to bed. The dog and I would settle down nearby. The coals smouldered and glowed. Every few evenings I would bake two potatoes in the coals – one for me, one for the dog. When they were ready, we shared this tasty treat and life didn't seem so bad after all.

The school's New Year break was drawing near, and my temporary release with it: I'd have two weeks to spend with my grandmother and step-grandfather. At school I had a couple of friendly schoolmates to return to. And a half-year of exile with my mother was over.

After receiving our report cards, we got ready for a carnival. Uncharacteristically, my mother decided to join in. She mixed some dyes in a pail, tied knots in the corners of a sheet and soaked it. When it was dry, she folded the sheet in half, sewed up the sides, cut out a hole at the top, and the result was an unusual and splendid sack dress. Then she sat me down near the kitchen window and, pulling a few things from her nearly empty cosmetics bag, she began to make me up. We rarely touched each other. Yet now her fingers slid over my forehead, she patted down my nose and cheeks, gave finishing touches to my eyelids, chin and eyebrows. Her hands and clothes smelled of medicine, which was my mother's usual fragrance. That smell, along with her touch, awakened in me a love I had not felt before: love for my mother.

When she handed me the mirror, a child's face glared back at me that was divided between good and evil. The fearful grimace on one side was set off by a black furrow that ran from my nose to my chin and a still-blacker eyebrow. The other side was as if sprinkled with gold powder, bright with a happy mouth, its corners turned up. 'Who am I?' I asked my mother. 'A split personality,' she replied.

In school, getting lost in a crowd of elves, rabbits, squirrels, Snow Whites and gingerbread men, I felt myself admired. I did not win the prize for the best costume, but in my heart I felt that the Split Personality had won.

Joyfully, I ran home in the late evening. Maybe my mother would be waiting and dinner would be ready. The next day I would be leaving for two weeks. I wanted to put my arms around her neck and kiss her in thanks for this beautiful carnival, for the Split Personality, which she had conjured up like a miracle worker.

Outside the house a frenzied dog was waiting for me instead. Inside was dark and cold. Neither the pot-bellied stove nor the cooking stove had been fired up. From the corridor, I could hear strange wheezing. My mother was lying in bed, beside her a bottle of alcohol and some white tablets. Around her neck was an old man's necktie, with which she had tried to strangle herself. I rushed to her, tore off that damned necktie and propped her up. She choked and coughed, then vomited up a liquid with more of those white tablets floating in it. All night I brewed tea for her. She obediently drank it, and vomited now and then. When she fell asleep, I crawled in beside her. I slept, hardly breathing, my head pressed to her left breast, to be sure that her heart was still beating.

*

Serafima didn't come to see me for at least a week. I didn't look for her. Larisa Nikolayevna told me that Serafima's husband was in hospital. A drinking buddy had attacked him in the stairwell. Otherwise everything was peaceful. We continued our research at the Institute. The first snow of winter left a thin layer of white on the bumpy pavements and the shabby rooftops. The Neva had not yet frozen over. Edged in white, the bridges looked romantic. Christmas was just around the corner and I recalled the windows in our old Riga flat covered with heavy blankets, my mother lighting candles on the tree and, with my stepfather, quietly, practically whispering, singing the carol:

Es skaistu rozīt' zinu	Lo, how a rose e'er blooming
No sīkas saknītes,	From tender stem hath sprung
Tā rozīt', ko es minu	Of Jesse's lineage coming,
No Jeses cēlusies...	As men of old have sung...

Celebrating Christmas was prohibited. The Christian holiday was replaced by fireworks, by the many clocks on the Kremlin chiming in the New Year, and an announcer's voice proclaiming in Russian, '*S novym godom, tovarish-chi! S novym schastyem!*' – 'Happy New Year, comrades! Here's to new happiness!'

I walked along the snow-covered Neva bridge and quietly sang, '*Es skaistu rozīt zinu.*' We all used to think that Jesse in this hymn meant Jesus. Such a miraculous story, believable only if one had faith. My mother and my stepfather had never talked about Jesus. I read about him in the old professor's books, the ones I had lugged up to my room from the pile discarded in our yard.

But medicine had outpaced Jesus. Everything was explicable and understandable. There was no need for faith. And Jesus had been prohibited. In His place, we were to believe in a real 'lotus-land' – that is, in Communism, under which everything would belong to everyone and euphoria would reign. For the time being, nothing indicated that this had been achieved. Already thirty years had passed since the war, but no one was complaining. The words of a Soviet song fitted our idyllic view of the world:

Varen plaša mana zeme dzimtā, lauki, meži, saules staru plīvs. Un es nezinu starp zemēm simtām, kur vēl citur cilvēks ir tik brīvs.

Mighty vast my land of birth, its fields and forests, rippling sunbeams. Of hundreds of other lands, I don't know anywhere man can be so free.

But for a short while Jesse – Jesus – lifted me away from this, my destined time and place, away from the life into which I had mistakenly been born. My birth obliged me to be alive: an absurd happenstance. There were so many who more than anything had wished to live but hadn't been born. Who decided this?

That evening I noticed that my women colleagues were oddly quiet and reserved with me. The usual joking around and tall stories were missing. Missing too were our usual evening drinks. The next morning

I learned why. In the corridor two men dressed identically were waiting for me. I had to leave the Institute without delay to return to Riga and there meet with my head doctor.

Crying, Larisa Nikolayevna helped me to pack. I described the men to her. I confessed that it was I who had beaten Serafima's husband. And that I didn't regret it. Larisa Nikolayevna was convinced that this was the last time she would ever see me and that I would be arrested on the train or possibly at Riga's railway station.

I was surprised how calm and fearless I felt. So this was what the end of the road would be like. No one was waiting for me at the station. I took my place in a second-class carriage, where the passengers were already unpacking their bundles of hard-boiled eggs, bread, sausage and pickles. The attendant was jangling glasses of tea in their filigree metal holders. As the train began to move, savoury aromas wafted about and I politely refused several offers of food. When all grew quiet, the aroma of food gave way to that of sweat. I walked out into the corridor to smoke. The train sped along and the night sped with it. This might be the last free night of my life. It was taking me back to my tenuous roots – to my mother, my stepfather and daughter. I had betrayed them. I was returning as one driven away, sooner or later to be stoned. I hoped they would arrest me at Riga station and so save me from confronting my family.

On returning to my seat, I slept for a brief while. The din of the train rocked me. In my dream I saw my father. The newspapers that always littered his room had been organized into a large black-and-white cross. He lay there with his eyes open, breathing in and out heavily. I approached him and said, 'Close your eyes, you're dead.' He continued to breathe, wordlessly confirming that he was alive.

At Riga station too I found no one waiting for me. A holiday mood was in the air. Spruce trees were being sold in the station square. I took the third tram to reach my meeting with the head doctor. Riga seemed like a dishonoured young girl, her head hung low in the tranquil, late-December air. People in long queues outside shops shifted from foot to foot. On a corner mandarins were being sold. The lucky ones got to buy them by the kilogram. The year 1977 was giving way to 1978. On festive tables you would be sure to find potato salad and sausage, and *Sovetskoye shampanskoye* – Soviet champagne. Life trapped inside this bubble would keep on at its established pace. I was hoping they would arrest me at the head doctor's office.

In the hospital corridor the head doctor didn't greet me, just nodded for me to enter his office. He locked the door. Then he sat down at his large desk, glaring, and pounded his fist on the table.

'You've destroyed not only your career but mine too. I put in a good word on your behalf. I was interrogated about you. A doctor, a woman, a mother, beats up an ex-soldier and hero of the Great Patriotic War. How do you justify your actions?'

'He beat his wife, whom we had succeeded in impregnating.'

'What did you succeed in?' The head doctor's face turned deep red in his fury.

'We impregnated his wife, because he couldn't manage it. She brought the sperm, we warmed it and injected it into her.'

'Do you understand the line you have crossed? You are banished. You won't get work in any of the city's hospitals. And you can thank that ex-soldier of the Great Patriotic War, since he signed a request that you should not be criminally prosecuted. You deserve to be. You deserve to be put in prison.'

'I would like to be in prison.'

'You're not normal and I don't understand why God has given you such talent.'

'God, as you know, doesn't exist.'

'Out of my sight! Get out! Get out!'

I walked out into the corridor and drew into my lungs the familiar smell of disinfectant and medication. I was banished from my paradise. Prison would have been my redemption. Nothing made sense any more.

*

Gradually I got used to my new life, to my mother's good and bad moments, and stays with my grandparents that were marked by sad farewells. I was still young, but I sensed that on the inside I was growing up. I was responsible for my mother. No one knew her light and dark sides better than I did. No one else stood ready to catch the next moment when she would want to leave her life behind.

Sometimes she would come home unexpectedly early, roast a crackling chicken and bake a delicious apple cake. We would eat while the dog waited under the table for tasty morsels. My mother would tell me strange stories, things no one had ever told me before. She said that we had once been free. I didn't understand. We'd had our own nation. But we have our own nation, I protested: the Soviet Union. Before it was only Latvia, my mother said. Her face took on that familiar, fearful grimace. There was only Latvia, she repeated, without the Russian lice, which won't live in their own homeland but crawl all over us. In our school there were two classes of Latvians and one of Russians, and we got along well. Why lice?

We country children were all equal. In summer at the *kolkhoz* we would squat with sunburned backs and soil-covered feet and hands in infinitely long beetroot and cucumber rows. We weeded and counted the endless metres remaining until we met a quota approved by a fierce woman brigadier. If she found even one weed, you had to weed another portion. In the autumn, school began after the harvest. First the vegetables had to be dug out with pitchforks and piled up, then their tops had to be cut or twisted off. Sometimes it was freezing, other times it rained. But we continued to cut and twist. Our young proletariat worked their fingers to the bone. Freedom was that tiny glimmer of happiness when, soaked through, we would drag ourselves home and dry out beside a hot stove, fortified by fresh clothes and dinner.

'They're raising new slaves,' my mother used to say. What she said often seemed incomprehensible to me – about freedom, and the lice and the slaves. I became used to her living in her own world, which I accepted in our calm coexistence. At school I did not talk about life at home, which was so different from the lives of my school friends.

One morning something strange happened in our small village. Nearby, on the high street, someone had scrawled in chalk: 'Let's grind the Russians into flour – that'll fulfil our food quota.'

An investigation was launched at school. Everyone denied everything. The Russian class viewed everyone else with suspicion. Rumours circulated that the culprit was one of the grown-ups.

After two days, I was called out of class to the headmistress's office. Beside the head sat a man in a grey coat. The head told me that the comrade wished to talk to me.

A feeling of deep dread rose inside me. I was terrified that I would be left alone with this comrade in the headmistress's office. I must have turned so pale that the headmistress made me sit down and poured me a glass of water. 'Your heart is pounding,' she said. 'Maybe we should call the school nurse? Maybe later?' She looked at the comrade, who sat at her desk unperturbed, drumming on it with his fat fingers. 'No, now. Leave,' he said to the head harshly.

We were alone in the office. The comrade grabbed my shoulder and painfully yanked me around to face him.

'Now stop shaking and answer my questions,' he said. 'Has your mother ever told you anything that is not taught in school?'

I started to cry. And in an instant I understood that the only ones suspected of the chalk graffiti on the street were my mother and me.

'Calm down and answer my question. Unless you answer you will not leave this room,' the comrade shouted.

Then, to my own surprise, I did calm down. I took a deep breath and said, 'Yes, she did tell me how a baby is created. She's a doctor, she knows this, and now I also know. That's not taught in school.'

The comrade looked as if he'd been dunked in icy water. My fear was receding. In its place grew a feeling that there was nothing he could do to me. He would never, under any circumstances, find out what I knew: about freedom, about the lice and the slaves. He would never find out.

The comrade looked uncomfortable.

'Is that all she's told you?'

'No, not all. She's drawn how a baby lies in a mother's womb and how hard it is for it to get out. And in general, how hard it is to be born.'

I took heart. I saw how the comrade's sweaty countenance deflated. How he pulled out his dirty handkerchief and wiped his face.

'Great strength is needed,' I said, 'for the baby to crawl out of its mother. Usually that takes place with his or her head first.'

'Thanks, that's enough,' the comrade said. 'I have no more questions.'

He stood, opened the door and called in the head, who had been waiting obediently outside.

'Everything is in order,' the comrade said.

I saw enormous relief in the headmistress's eyes. She led me back out into the corridor, told me that I could have the rest of the day off and patted my head quite kindly.

I snatched my school bag from the classroom and my coat from the locker and headed for my beloved embankment by the railway tracks.

I settled down on a tree stump. This was my freedom, my time. From afar an overnight train roared its approach. Those trains never stopped at our station.

When the din of the train had faded, silence set in. In that silence, my heart beat calmly and I feared neither the dark forest nor the animals it harboured. And I wasn't afraid of my mother, only terribly worried about her. And I knew it would be like this until death separated us.

It was a strange evening. I boiled a pail of water, got an old brush and went out into the street. The dog followed me. I poured hot water over the chalked graffiti and, with alternate sluicing and scrubbing, the words gradually disappeared. Now and then, lights in the surrounding houses marked out curious onlookers, but no one stared for long. Even after darkness fell, I continued to scrape away at the asphalt with my brush. When I finally went home, all that remained was a blurred chalk residue.

*

Exiled, I went out into the hospital's car park. At intervals the ambulances would bring new patients to the emergency entrance. I gazed at the lighted windows. The dimly lit wards, the bright lights of the operating theatre, the dark blue of the morgue. All these were mine no longer. I was driven out into a world for which I cared nothing. A world in which I had been unnecessary since birth.

I inhaled smoke deeply into my lungs. I wanted to draw out this moment before I'd have to go home and face my mother, stepfather and daughter. I wanted to delay seeing their bewildered faces, half-happy perhaps, but mostly reflecting the shadow of fear. Their calm lives would be subjected to the unknown once more. It was snowing lightly. I decided to make a detour. Along Miera Street as far as Lenin Street. Maybe somewhere there would be mandarins for sale.

On Lenin Street blue stars were twinkling. The city was being decorated for the New Year celebrations. Opposite the brightly lit Riga Fashion salon I was overcome by a desire to have my hair washed and styled. Inside, hairdressers were rushing around a few well-tended, fragrant women. I stood there clutching my old suitcase, reeking of cigarettes and the hospital. Beneath my hat, tied with elastic, my hair had gone several days without washing and had never been coloured. No one paid any attention to me. I stood there for a moment longer, then walked out. It had been an idiotic impulse.

Thinking of Serafima, I stopped at the St Alexander Nevsky Orthodox Church. Did she tell her abusive husband the truth? Did she suffer because of that truth? Would she be able to protect her child?

I crossed the street and walked past Café Flora. The majority of us medical students had no time to sit in such freethinker cafés. Our days were spent in auditoriums, our evenings and nights in the anatomy lab. Idling in a café seemed like a foolish waste of time.

At the crossing, a granite Vladimir Ilyich Lenin greeted me. Lenin had cooked up all of this bitter misery, and for more than half a century thousands had had to stomach it. I was born into this mess and I would have to die in it. I didn't even have the memories that my parents had. My father used to talk about the time when Latvia was independent, and about the Milk restaurant, which stood where the Hotel Latvia now reached for the sky. He and my mother had met there during a break between lectures and had a delicious meal. And then they had taken a walk around the nearby Freedom Monument, which was known as Milda. This was separated from Lenin's statue by a lime tree-lined avenue, and the statues had their backs to each other. For one *lats* a street photographer had taken a picture of my mother and father standing beside Milda.

Lenin had also turned his back on the Orthodox cathedral, which had been converted into a planetarium. It was a civilized gesture, as if he knew nothing of the distant lake in Siberia where, on his orders, hundreds of Orthodox priests had been drowned.

Yes, God doesn't exist. I had already confirmed that. But there is a heaven and there are stars. And I had been driven out of my paradise.

I stepped inside the planetarium to get warm. To one side was *Dieva auss* – God's Ear. This was another café that I hadn't managed to visit as a student. I ordered coffee with a shot of Balsam spirit. The patrons around me looked relaxed. They were sitting on the floor. Some were throwing matchboxes around. Maybe it was a game known only to them. Cigarette smoke curled in the air.

I sat in a corner and truly felt that I was in this nonexistent God's ear. I had wandered in there on the way out of my paradise. A gaunt man with long hair approached my table. He had ordered two more Balsam shots and wished to get acquainted. He claimed to be thirty-three – the same age as Jesus when he died.

'That's my age too,' I said. 'Is Jesse only a man's name?' I asked, having privately already baptized him 'Jesse', like in the Christmas hymn.

'That's a brave question,' he responded. 'What do you do for a living?'

'I was a doctor,' I said.

'And what now?'

'Do we have any idea of what comes next? Is there any sense, living here, in thinking about what's next?'

'You have a point,' Jesse agreed keenly. 'Living here, there's little sense to life. The world goes on outside. For a whole decade, while we cowards sit in these cafés,' he whispered, '*they* are dying for us.'

'Who are they?' I whispered back.

'Jan Palach, who in 1969 set fire to himself and died in the centre of Prague.'

'My daughter was born in '69,' I told Jesse.

He seemed not to hear and continued: 'Janis Joplin and Jimmy Hendrix – they overdosed in '70. For their and our freedom.' Jesse's voice grew louder. 'For freedom in general, understand? And also Jim Morrison, the very next year. While we putrefy here and pretend to be underground heroes. There's nothing real here, either on the streets or in the cafés. Everywhere's just a pitiful existence. Everyone everywhere is pretending, not living. On the streets pretending to be obedient Soviet citizens and here we pretend to be dissidents. There's no freedom here.'

I listened to Jesse, to the names which meant nothing to me. I only knew two irrefutable facts about this period: a daughter had been born to me, and recently at the physiology laboratory in Cambridge a woman's ovum had been artificially fertilized, which I had discovered from a journal sent by my uncle from London in a parcel of clothes.

Jesse – I wanted to interject into this whispered flood of words – Jesse, do you even realize what that means?

There's no mystery, there's no divine will. Nor is there any freedom – either to be born or to die. This medical manipulation proves that.

But Jesse grew tipsy and continued to whisper about freedom snatched from us and someone living and dying for us.

Eventually, his whisper died away. Jesse crossed his hands, let his head droop and fell asleep. His long hair spread across gaunt shoulders.

I quietly stood up and left God's Ear.

*

A glass of warm milk and over it a freshly formed skin. Milk soup. Fruit jelly in milk. Those were my worst trials at school. In our country school drinking milk was obligatory. I hated milk and all that was associated with it. I struggled with it as if with an invisible devil trying to possess me, no matter how hard I resisted. I tried to drink it in great gulps, not breathing through my nose, so as not to taste it. After drinking my glass of milk, as often as not I would rush to the school toilet and try to make myself sick.

My school day was divided into pre-milk and post-milk. The pre-milk time just before lunch was unbearable. I had trouble concentrating. Flashing before my eyes were – not continents or pistils and stamens, not catheti or hypotenuses, but glasses of milk. In the afternoon, however, I was attentive and observant. I could work out a square root and recognize a double infinitive. Everything fell into place as soon as that damned taste of milk disappeared from my mouth. Unfortunately, my battle with milk became ever more noticeable, until the teacher wrote in my daily journal that my mother should come in for a meeting.

I dragged myself home like a whipped dog. My mother and I lived separate lives. It wasn't good to get her involved in my milk secret. Now it couldn't be helped.

The next afternoon, during biology, I saw through the window my mother approaching the school. She was wearing a flimsy coat and a crocheted beret. I saw how she stopped before the flowerbeds to light a cigarette. She had become one with her cigarettes. Our clothes were always permeated with the stench of cigarette smoke. In a strange way I preferred this to the smell of milk.

It was so unusual to see my mother at the school. For others it was a customary occurrence because parents still came to get their children – because of the dark road and the graveyard, which frightened us. I pictured how it would be if she was waiting for me, for her daughter. It was a good feeling. My mother is different. But she is my mother and she's waiting for me after school. The teacher was saying something about monocotyledonous and dicotyledonous plants, but out there by the flower-beds my mother stood waiting for me.

The bell rang. A happy stream of students flowed out of school, ready to fall into their parents' embraces and go home to warm dinners. My mother and I didn't know how to behave. I went up to her, put my arms around her, the way the others did, and for a brief while we stood like that. Then I took her by the hand and led her inside. The corridors were empty, the cafeteria tidied but still saturated with the smell of milk. The teacher's office was past the cafeteria. She asked my mother to come in and told me to wait outside. I might as well have gone in too, because the acoustics in the empty spaces carried almost every word the teacher said to my ears.

'Have you noticed her dislike of milk?'

'We don't have milk at home.'

'But it's necessary for a growing child's organism. In school she manages to pour out her daily glass of milk, or give it to a classmate or gulp it down then run to the toilet. Does that seem normal to you?'

'Maybe she has an allergy to milk.'

'Don't make me laugh. You're a doctor. Is there such a thing as an allergy to milk, the healthiest and most noble of foods? Do you not, as a mother, fear that without milk she might not develop fully?'

'Maybe it's because she never received her mother's milk.'

'Why is that? Did you have some sort of illness?'

'Yes. I didn't want to live, and I didn't want her to have milk from a mother who didn't want to live.'

The clock ticked in the empty lunch room. It ticked so loudly that I felt compelled to count the ticks. Beyond the windows pigeons were flapping in the puddles. The milk smell had permeated the lunch-room tables, chairs and walls. And the silence was unbearable. I waited for the teacher to throw my mother out of her office.

'I won't tell anyone what you've just told me. The consequences could be unpredictable. Please talk to your daughter about the milk. We don't want to torture the child.'

The door opened and the teacher's face showed an expressive grimace: you poor, poor child. My mother and I politely said our goodbyes.

Outside, spring was in the air. Immediately my mother lit a cigarette. How greedily she inhaled and exhaled the smoke into the fresh air! We walked in silence but my heart was skipping joyfully. I was walking home from school with my mother. I wanted this road to go on for ever. If it went on for ever, we could walk in silence and we could talk. Both would be good.

'Let's take a detour,' my mother said, as if reading my thoughts.

We turned off onto the old road that led towards the river. There, to the left of the avenue, stretched a field with an old wooden house at its far edge. Everyone knew that its owner was not quite sane and therefore kept a safe distance from the house. But my mother grasped my hand firmly and led me directly into that fearful zone. There was no one in the house. We could hear cows mooing in the barn. We followed the sound, despite my terrible misgivings. Sitting in there, her eyes like two black dots behind thick glasses, was the old lady, milking her cows. The warm milk was trickling into a pail. I started to feel nauseous and tried to pull away from my mother's hand, but she held me firmly. The owner of the house poured what she had just milked from the pail into a jar and placed a cup beside it.

'Drink, child,' she said, like the youngest of all the witches in my fairy tales.

'Drink, child,' my mother repeated. 'Drink,' she said again, sensing my increasing resistance.

'Well, then. When I die, then you'll see!' Crying and almost gagging, I drank the warm milk. My tears added salt to the milk. I gulped it down so that the battle would be over.

In the evening my mother gave me a signed letter addressed to my teacher, requesting that they not force me to drink milk. My fury melted into gratitude.

The next morning, the familiar nausea had disappeared. Visions of milk no longer obsessed me instead of continents, stamens, catheti and hypotenuses. At lunch, no one put a glass in front of me. But I tasted a little of my neighbour's milk. It was the same milk that I couldn't stand, but I could drink it or not. I had gained a little freedom.

*

Often my patients had not made a choice to have a child or not to have one. Whether for lovers who refused to accept a pregnancy or husbands who didn't want the burden of more children, the exhausted women capitulated. They were ready to endure inhuman abortion pains without anaesthesia. And opposite them in the corridor sat another endless line desperate for children – but a child wouldn't come no matter how hard they tried.

In the long hours of waiting outside my consultation room the women sometimes managed to bare their hearts to one another. It was all the fault of men, asking women to give up their child, or not allowing them to get pregnant. Yet men themselves were indifferent. They considered this part of women's world. And Soviet medicine would take care of them.

I sat in my country ambulatory centre in the narrow room with its dilapidated wood stove, its ancient gynaecological chair and suspect examination instruments. This was Soviet medicine.

I often thought of Serafima, now no more than a vague image from a world whose door was unconditionally closed to me. Once she came to me in a dream and said that she had lost her child after all. She had the same lovely face but her eyes were closed. She spoke with her eyes closed. I woke in a cold sweat. And I tried to comfort myself that maybe it meant exactly the opposite, as quite often happens with dreams. White is black and black is white. Life is death, death is life. The narrow corridor of the small ambulatory centre, where my women sit day after day in a never-ending queue, is proof of that.

It was an ordinary late afternoon. Countless incomplete patients' record cards lay on my chaotic desk, along with a half-drunk cup of coffee, an ashtray and a number of microscope slides with smears which were to be packed up and sent to the nearest city lab. A lamp with its quivering light, a pile of firewood by the stove, an oilcloth screen and a narrow leatherette couch. The familiar, annoying sound of a knock at the door.

I knew what I would see when I opened the door. They would continue to sit and wait. Patiently, eternally, with no end in sight.

After a short pause I opened the door. There it was – the long line of waiting women, and at the end of the line, her knees carefully squeezed together, with her school bag on her shoulders, sat my daughter. She had come to meet me.

Thus she sat there, not realizing what this queue was for. Nor that sooner or later she too would have reason to join the others. Nor that no one, including me, knew how she would fare in the queue or if she would choose it for herself. She had braided her hair herself and clumsily tied blue ribbons in it.

Patiently she awaited the end of my working day. We locked up the ambulatory centre and went home. 'It will be cold at home,' said my daughter. 'The dog will definitely be sleeping in my bed.' It had iced over and the snow crunched under our feet. 'Let's go to that hill where we can see the sky over the river,' she said suddenly. I lit a cigarette. All around was silent and dark. Somewhere a dog began to bark. We walked through the old graveyard. 'Now it's safe,' she said. Among the grey and black tombstones glimmered white grave mounds. The moonlight shone at a slant and the shadows thrown by the cedars lay across the blanket of snow. 'Now it's safe,' my daughter said again, and took my mitten-clad hand.

The hillside began beyond the graveyard. The snow came up to our knees. There were no other footprints or visible path. Short of breath, I stopped halfway. I lit a cigarette. She stopped to wait for me. Then she started to trudge in front, creating footprints for me to walk in. My daughter walked vigorously in front of me, her braids covered with hoarfrost and on her back her school bag swinging to and fro.

We stopped at the brow of the hill. Below us was a small, steep slope, edged with protecting trees. It shone in the white moonlight.

'Look how beautifully the heavenly bodies shine!' said my daughter.

Over the river the sky was full of stars. And plumb in the middle gazed the round face of the moon.

Behind us stretched the line of my daughter's footprints, by which I had climbed up the hill. In front lay a virgin, snow-clad field.

*

It was a school holiday. Everyone was preparing for the jubilee of the Great October Socialist Revolution, which of course nowadays is celebrated in November. That year November had arrived almost unnoticed. I wasn't able to visit my grandmother and step-grandfather that autumn break. My mother wasn't feeling well. She only just managed to keep going to work at the ambulatory centre. In the evenings she would be asleep early. All the household chores fell to me. No matter how much I yearned for my grandparents, I would not leave my mother by herself. I had washed and ironed my own white blouse, but I was worried about the hole in my red pioneer neckerchief: it was too small to be mended but still noticeable. I decided to tuck the neckerchief into my blue vest, as if unintentionally. And in the solemn student council line I took care never to stand in the front row. The main thing was to salute properly and yell clearly, '*Vienmēr gatavs!*' – 'Always ready!' And never to forget this rallying song:

Kreiso, kreiso,	Left, left,
Kreiso, kreiso!	Left, left!
Pašā Rīgas vidū	In Riga's very centre
Piemineklis stalts.	A stately monument.
Granīts brūni sarkans,	In granite brownish red,
Ļeņins bronzā kalts.	Lenin in bronze is forged.
Kreiso, kreiso,	Left, left,
Kreiso, kreiso!	Left, left!

That morning, my mother sat on the edge of her bed, rummaging through her handbag, looking for her tablets. Sometimes I would help her, picking them out of the lining. This time I couldn't find anything, so we hunted for them together. My mother looked so helpless. I brewed a strong coffee for her, hoping that it would help. With a large mug of coffee and her first cigarette, my mother revived. She shooed me out to school so I wouldn't be late.

All the female teachers had voluminous backcombed hairdos. They had dressed up in suits and high heels. Outside, the school flew our great motherland's flag. We sang the hymn. The first verse was my favourite:

> We've gained freedom for this land most dear.
> Generation after generation born happy we'll be.
> Here our sea soughs, our tilled fields flower.
> Here our cities shine, here Riga resounds.

And the refrain, in which the singers dwelt passionately on the first word:

> So—o—oviet Latvia, may she live for ever.
> May she brightly in the Soviet wreath shine.

I didn't understand the next verse, which proclaimed our comradeship with the sublime Russian nation, which would conquer our enemies. Who were our enemies?

The third verse and refrain completed the hymn. Mechanically, I fulfilled all the required actions. I sang along with the others, but I was thinking only of my mother. I was filled with foreboding.

Kreiso, kreiso!

I remembered the drawing that my mother had made in our city flat with me sitting in her lap.

Kreiso, kreiso!

The mother with her baby, united by an umbilical cord and their mutual happiness.

Kreiso, kreiso!

There was no joy here. I was counting the seconds to when this solemn parade with all its rallying cries and songs would be over. When it was, I would pull on my coat and hurry home. Then maybe a miracle would happen and everything would be OK. My mother would be at work, or maybe at home and waiting for me with roast chicken and apple cake.

Kreiso, kreiso!	Left, left!
Vienmēr gatavs!	Always ready!
Brīvi!	At ease!

Finally! Once out of the auditorium, I raced like the wind to my locker in the corridor, pulled on my coat and rushed home.

My mother was lying in bed as white as a sheet. I couldn't feel her breath. I pressed on her heart with both hands and blew my breath into her mouth. That's what we were taught in school with a blown-up rubber doll.

'*Kreiso, kreiso!*' I cried out, through my tears, and went on trying to breathe for her.

'*Kreiso, kreiso!*'

Suddenly my mother wheezed deeply, and under my hands I felt her heart violently begin to beat again. The wheezes subsided into fairly steady breathing. I threw back the blanket, since she seemed desperate for air. The linen was wet beneath her. I had to change her clothes and the sheet in a hurry, so she wouldn't catch cold. And I had to fire up the wood stove.

*

This was deeper than sleep, deeper than dreams. It was as if I were gliding through scenes from my life. My mother was ironing a school apron. My stepfather was making paper covers for my notebooks. Suddenly my daughter was wading through a snow-covered field, and I wanted to follow in her footsteps, but I was always too late and missed them. Then my father was cutting down the stand of saplings, and I wanted to run to him, to tell him to come to his senses, but I couldn't, because it seemed I had no legs.

Serafima appeared in the white light. She was naked and beautiful. Her skin was smooth and glowing, her breasts were supple and round, her legs slim, covered with a light, white down. She was so appealing, so yielding. I went to her and kissed the tiny hollow in her neck. My sense of smell was as acute as a dog's. I was hypersensitive, as if overheated in the sun. Serafima responded to my kiss, she touched my breasts, they tensed and yielded to her hands. Serafima's hands were cool and slid easily over my shoulders, arms and thighs. She unwrapped the shawl in which for some reason I had been wound. I was a cocoon, seeing in front of me a beautiful, splendid butterfly – Serafima.

She had half-uncovered me, and I felt a coolness. She embraced me, and suddenly from her flesh to mine flowed a tender wave of warmth. It seemed to wind around me more closely than the shawl. I heard my own heart and pulse, but maybe it was Serafima's pulse. The two beats mingled together. Gratefully, I dropped to my knees and embraced her smooth legs.

There was neither suffering nor hardship. Life, with all its pitiful daily burdens, was somewhere far behind. Was this dying? Such a sensation of happiness, granted to compensate for all the torment on earth. I wanted this moment to last for ever – the pulse at my temple against Serafima's legs. But someone with unbelievable strength was pulling me away from her. I couldn't resist. And Serafima didn't help me. She stood there splendid and unmoving. But I hung on tightly, ever so tightly, to her knees, her calves, her ankles, her toes, until she slid out of my grasp, because I hadn't the strength to resist. I slipped away from her. Serafima was left in the white light with my shawl in her hands. Life's quagmire drew me back.

*

67

My mother got well quickly. For about a week a nurse from the ambulatory centre came to our house and gave her an injection. Each time the nurse came she sighed profoundly, saying to my mother that she should get on her feet soon because her patients were continually asking for her. My mother's consulting room was full of sweets and flowers. Should she bring them here for her? 'No,' said my mother. 'Divide them among our colleagues.'

I cared for my mother as best I could. She wrote a note requesting that I be excused from school. In the mornings, sitting on my mother's bed, we breakfasted together. At midday we ate a lunch that I prepared. Dinner we just had snacks. Mother read to me from her books. From *Moby-Dick*, of course. 'Call me Ishmael,' she exclaimed in a feeble voice before each reading. I didn't understand the ungodly God-like man, monomaniacal Captain Ahab, and his obsession with the white whale. In my opinion it was a doom-filled book. But it visibly cheered my mother.

My mother's return to daily life was a good time. She smoked less and didn't take any tablets, at least in my presence. Her interest in food returned and, probably for the first time, she praised me for the meals I made. 'Who taught you this?' she asked, savouring a casserole or sipping a soup. 'How did you figure this out? Well yes, you're a big girl now. Are you already thirteen?'

During our leisure time, a schoolmate arrived with news that a monument was being unveiled in our village. Right by the railway station, not far from my beloved embankment by the tracks. It turned out that more than fifty years ago in our undistinguished country station a Russian diplomatic courier had been killed. He had become a hero in Russia, and therefore now also a hero in Latvia. My mother dismissed all this as bootlicking. That was a favourite expression of hers. I had several questions for her. Who and why would someone do that? My mother explained that when Latvia was free, you didn't have to lick Russia's boots. 'Now we have to erect a monument to some dubious spy.'

I didn't understand what she was talking about. I had a much bigger task to think about than our enchained Latvia. For the monument's unveiling I was to recite a stanza from Vladimir Mayakovsky's poem 'The Boat', which he had dedicated to the railway station's hero. Although I was assiduously attempting to learn Russian, reciting by heart was daunting! I begged my mother to help me. So for several days our reading time began with 'Call me Ishmael' and ended with my desperate attempts to remember the stanza and my mother's sarcastic comments:

> *My zhivyom, zazhatye zheleznoy klyatvoy*
> We live with a cast-iron oath on our lips
> *Za neyo na krest, i puleyu cheshite.*
> For this oath we would give away bullets.
> *Cheshite, cheshite.*
> Away, away.

(Mother: Let him go away for once!)

Eto, chtoby v mire bez Rossiy, bez Latviy
   So that this world beyond Russia and Latvia
Zhit yedinym chelovechynim obshchezhityem.
   Would be a single common abode.

(Mother: This he said well – humanity's communal flat!)

V nashikh zhilakh krov, a ne voditsa.
   In our veins blood, not water.
My idyom skvoz revolverny lay.
   We walk through the sound of shooting.

(Mother: Dogs, Russian dogs!)

Chtobi umiraya voplotitsa
   So on dying we may become
V parakhodi, v strochki i v drugiye dolgiye dela.
   Boats, lines of poetry and other eternal things.

'Call me Ishmael!'

In a strange way my mother's comments helped me remember this taxing combination of words and lines, and the pronunciation, which was tying my Latvian tongue in knots. The hardest thing to say in Russian was the term for dormitory, *chelovechynim obshchezhityem*, which was almost as hard as our Latvian term for narrow-gauge railway, *šaursliežu dzelzceļš*. My mother began to like this game. She started to teach me to add emotion to my reciting. She parodied a man's deep voice and soon we were doubled over in giggles. In the end I was heartily grateful to Russia's diplomatic courier for getting shot precisely at our railway station, and even more grateful to Mayakovsky for giving my mother and me such moments of rare happiness.

I recited my stanza at the monument so enthusiastically that my Russian teacher broke down in tears, while my Latvian teacher hatched a plan to send me to the regional reciting competition.

I skipped home to my mother, splashing through the autumn leaves and loudly crowing, 'Call me Ishmael! Call me Ishmael!'

My mother wasn't at home. She was back chained to her ambulatory centre. I happily fed the dog, lit the wood stove and began to peel potatoes. I felt a cold draught from Mother's room, where she had left the window open. An ashtray lay on the bed beside *Moby-Dick*. In it was a bookmark. More precisely, it was a small piece of paper covered with fine print, torn out of a book. I examined it carefully, because I had never seen it in our house. There were also delicately printed numbers on the page. Beside the numbers eleven and twelve I read the following:

And the angel of the Lord said unto her, Behold, thou art with child and shalt bear a son, and shalt call his name Ishmael; because the Lord hath heard thy affliction.

And he will be a wild man; his hand will be against every man, and every man's hand against him; and he shall dwell in the presence of all his brethren.

Genesis 16: 11 - 12

*

They were strangely empty days and nights – when she went to stay with my mother and stepfather in the city. The dog wouldn't leave her room but stayed curled up on the rug under her desk. Everything seemed empty, cold and silent, and I would gladly have spent the night at the ambulatory centre. I never went with my daughter, because I didn't want to darken their meeting times, which were too brief already.

She usually visited them on Saturdays and Sundays. Time grew particularly burdensome on these days. I felt weighed down, as if I could never be free. Now and then I would go to the ambulatory centre, sit in my office and mechanically fill in the senseless record cards. Occasionally I stayed in bed for hours, smoking and reading, but everything seemed an aimless waste of time. Delivered on Fridays, the Russian medical journals could not cheer me. Soviet medical science was limping forward. Pitifully small advances could be gleaned from it. A façade obscured everything – the senseless party and regime proclamations, intended to demonstrate the regime's care for Soviet citizens, especially for its mothers and children:

Mothers who have given birth to and raised ten children shall be awarded the order 'Mother Hero', and mothers who have raised nine children will receive the order 'Mother Glory', mothers of six children will be awarded the 'Mother's Medal' Grade I. In socialist states all children have equal rights; these are not dependent on their ethnic origin, race, place of birth, economic status.

I never raised questions among my women patients, never counselled anyone to have an abortion. But giving birth and letting a child enter this world in this time and place seemed to me as senseless as everything else that was going on around us. We were cut off from the world. We were destined for a somnambulant existence and condemned to call it life. And I found myself at the heart of this somnambulism. I, one of the rank and file, day after day promoting and pursing senselessness.

But I wasn't thinking straight. Who else but my daughter could shine a beam of light into this sleepwalking existence? She suffered this exile at my side. Driven from a brilliant Soviet medical career, from its congresses, its bribes and backhanders. Excluded from science and its wondrous future discoveries. Banned from taking part in the most amazing discovery of all: human fertilization outside the human body.

During these empty days I had time to dwell. Scenes from the past resurfaced. I remembered my father telling me that he and my mother had had several opportunities to leave Latvia for Germany at the end of the war. Mother had been eight months pregnant with me. There was time before the Red Army invaded Riga. People were fleeing wherever they could, risking their lives, hiding in the forests by the sea, waiting for fishermen's boats bound for Gotland, in Sweden. My parents had had relatively safe opportunities to leave. But my mother had refused. She wanted her child to be born in her native land.

My mother's decision determined not only her life but also my father's life and mine. Unwittingly, I blamed her for everything. And I remembered myself at my daughter's age. When my mother used to weep in the kitchen every time she received the usual refusal to visit her brother in London, I didn't feel sorry for her at all. But, unlike me, she was such a good and caring mother. She cherished me – just as my daughter now cares for and cherishes me.

During those empty days I used to go into my daughter's room. There, in contrast to my chaos, everything was so touchingly neat. My mother's and stepfather's pictures in her handmade frames, propped against the old table lamp. A clay squirrel and a small clay dish, moulded with her own hands at a ceramics workshop. Her books and notebooks in neat piles; under the desk a bowl of water for the dog. My stepfather's sharpened coloured pencils in a wooden box, one of my medical encyclopedia volumes, with pressed flowers and herbs filling its pages, on the windowsill snail shells, which she had found on the riverbank. The old wardrobe, with her underwear and warm tights in neat piles in the drawers and, at the back, a hanger with her school uniform.

The dog wagged its tail politely, but continued to wait for her. I closed the door and went back to my smoke-filled room.

*

My mother rarely entered my room. Yet every time I returned from my grandparents, her fragrance seemed to linger there. Maybe she had slept in my bed for a while? I unpacked the washed and ironed laundry and prepared for the next school week. My mother almost never asked me how her mother and stepfather were. Just acknowledged their greetings to her.

I didn't tell my mother that her room in the flat had now been turned into mine. The books remaining from my mother's library had been neatly organized on shelves. On the day I arrived, a vase of flowers stood on the desk alongside a plate of tasty morsels. My grandmother had certainly aired the room, because the cigarette smell that used to permeate the sofa and large armchair was barely discernible. Now the curtains smelled of soap powder. My bed was always made up and on it a clean stack of the clothes and underwear that I had left the previous time.

Two days a week and for several days at a time during holidays I lived in this paradise. Later my room acquired a white hamster whom I named Bambi. He hated his cage. He used to race around in it like the devil faced with a cross. My presence meant Bambi's freedom. He was allowed to run around my room to his heart's content, leaving a trail of tiny droppings behind him. He used to wait for me, like waiting for an ally. Once Bambi disappeared for a whole night, and no matter how we called and looked he didn't respond or allow himself to be caught. In the morning our Polish neighbour from the floor below stood by our door holding Bambi. He had got into her toilet through the sewer pipe and was somewhat dazed and bruised. Holding him by the nape of the neck, my step-grandfather said, 'Old chap, we all have to live in a cage. Get used to it.'

When I arrived the next time, my grandmother had provided a lady friend for Bambi: a tiny brown hamster whom I named Rozālija Vējaslota – Rosie Tumbleweed. We hoped she would calm him down and help begin a serene family life in his cage. Rosie became pregnant. Bambi mostly slept indolently, curled in a corner of the cage. Rosie busied herself gathering shavings to make a nest. Bambi showed no further interest in her. The former freedom fighter was unrecognizable.

And then, on my next visit, something horrendous happened. Rosie's nest began to move and out tumbled the tiniest of tiny furless creatures, squeaking softly. On seeing them Bambi reared up on his back paws, shook himself and, grabbing the first newborn in his front paws like a carrot or a slice of potato, began to devour it, starting with its head. He was gobbling his own children, and with relish. My grandmother pulled Rosie's nest out of the cage, along with the rest of the squeakers. During the night they all died and, after a few days, so did Rosie. Gradually Bambi returned to his old ways. He lived for his free time outside the cage.

I despised Bambi. I wished he had died. What had he lacked in his cage? Food, a warm lair, a wife and children: had he ruined it all solely because he wanted to run around in my room?

I resolved not to let Bambi out of his cage ever. Week after week he waited for me, hoping for my mercy. I arrived, he reared up with his paws pressed against the cage bars and as good as beckoned to me: 'Please, please let me out.' But my heart had hardened.

One of the Sundays when I was leaving Riga spelled the end of Bambi. My grandmother said, 'He hasn't eaten for almost a week.' Curled up in a corner, he slept quietly. He'd lost his soft round tummy. When I entered the room, Bambi didn't react. There was none of the usual pleading ritual. I bent over the cage and saw that Bambi was breathing very feebly. He had hidden his tiny snout in his nest, his white fur coat moved weakly up and down. I felt sorry for him and opened the cage door. 'Bambi, you old monster. Come on out, let's race. Bambi, come out, there's freedom here.' But Bambi continued to sleep and breathe almost unnoticeably. After a moment, as I was watching, he convulsed and stiffened, his snout and paws turned rigid. Paying no attention to my grandmother's and step-grandfather's objections, I wrapped Bambi in a cloth napkin, then in a sack and the sack in my school bag. 'You don't have anywhere to bury him here,' I said, bid them goodbye and left for the station.

Outside the train window the stations trundled past one after the other. I wasn't thinking of the passengers, whom otherwise I would have looked over carefully to see if there wasn't some suspicious character among them. I didn't think about the path through the old graveyard, where I usually drew a deep breath and tried to race without looking to either side. I didn't even think about my grandparents, who were always on my mind when returning to my mother's. I would often start crying at that thought, pressing my nose against the train window. Instead I thought about Bambi, who, wrapped in the napkin, was going to his place of rest in the garden by our house. Where to bury him – under the apple tree or the jasmine, or simply by the fence – for the crime of devouring his children? Without a grave mound. Maybe I was to blame for his death. Most likely he died of his yearning for freedom. But had I sentenced him unjustly? How can one eat one's children and then die from yearning for freedom?

What usually seemed a long journey passed quickly this time. Our small station came along suddenly. It was nearly spring. In the evenings the light held for a long while. That meant I could walk in the graveyard unconcerned because it was still daylight. White anemones were blooming by the fence. Maybe Bambi should be buried right here in the graveyard? I wasn't brave enough for that. Besides, I wanted to show Bambi to my mother. Although Bambi didn't deserve flowers, I still picked a tiny bunch.

My mother was drinking coffee, smoking and reading in her room. Her window was open, overlooking the spring-like garden. She was happy to see me.

The dog sniffed at me. I unpacked my bag and took my bundle in to my mother's room. I said, 'Bambi died. Can we bury him in the garden?'

'What happened?' asked my mother.

'He ate his children and afterwards died longing for freedom,' I replied.

'A brave hamster,' my mother said.

'You call that brave?' I exclaimed, and all my suppressed tears – tears for leaving my grandparents, but also for losing Bambi, for our moments of freedom together – all my tears spilled out.

'Brave, you say? To eat his own children?' I cried inconsolably, struggling with the feelings of hate and love that were tearing me apart.

'By brave I meant his determination for freedom,' my mother said. 'Let's go and bury Bambi.'

My crying slowly calmed. We left the dog in the room and went out into the budding garden. Where, then? Under the jasmine or the apple tree, or simply by the fence for his sinful deed?

'You must forgive the dead,' said my mother. She took a spade and dug a small hole under the apple tree. I covered it with anemones and laid Bambi there. The white hamster lay among white flowers. Two strokes of the spade and he disappeared from our eyes, merging with the fragrant, black soil.

My mother lit a cigarette and for a while we lingered by Bambi's grave.

'But why did he eat his children?' I asked my mother.

'Probably he was saving them from being caged,' Mother said, and hugged me tightly. She was trembling all over, and her heart was beating violently. I hugged her back equally tightly. For a moment we stayed there. The aroma of the freshly dug soil mingled with the smell of cigarette smoke. Somewhere in the distance a nightingale twittered. Soon the cherries would blossom.

*

My tiny consulting room was slowly suffocating me. My patients multiplied. They circulated information about me and drove to see me from ever more distant regions, armed with flowers, boxes of sweets and fresh farm food. The overseers had forgotten about me, thinking that I was harmless in this far-flung place and that the penalty for my Leningrad 'crime' was severe enough.

My former city colleagues didn't seem to care how I was. In fact, they were afraid to show they cared and so risk ruining their blossoming and well-paid careers, now supplemented by trips to friendly USSR countries and even to the rotting West. They all knew that the penalty for contact with me would be a visit to the infamous corner building with its KGB overseers, its prison cells and pre-deportation holding tanks. Freedom had been dangled before me in the form of studies in Leningrad. I hadn't known how to deal with it. For this I'd been sent into exile in this stifling room at the ambulatory centre.

I had succeeded with my Serafima experiment several times. Women who couldn't get pregnant followed my instructions, brought me their husband's sperm, and the miracle, as they called it, happened. In their eyes, I became a miracle worker. But there was no miracle in this, just a casual, lucky happenstance, to which I lent my hand and some of the medical tricks I knew. Somehow, this tempered my sense of humiliation. It added up to more than the daily round of gynaecological examinations and diagnoses which I could do with such precision and ease that it felt like a game of patience. I shook a mental fist at the head doctor, who, in his gloomiest dreams, could never have envisaged that I, the exile, could repeat something like this.

Still, it's possible that exile saved me. I had experienced the death of only one patient. Had I remained in the meat-grinder that was Riga, I would have had to accept that patients' deaths are normal. An unavoidable medical statistic. I do remember the senselessness of that one death. The woman's labour pains had been dragging on, which in itself was not unusual. She was exhausted. Her pulse was weak and the baby's heartbeats ever fainter. I made the decision to do a caesarean section. In the operating room I was assisted by a student who still had much to learn. The anaesthesia took effect well. I did the section and took out a healthy, strong baby boy. I still needed to stitch the wound closed. I signalled to the student with my head that his help was no longer needed. Then, as I looked on, the student took his gloves off over the woman's open womb, and all the sweat-covered talc that was inside the gloves fell into the wound.

He stood there wide-eyed as the talc mixed with the woman's blood, stunned by what he had done. I threw myself at the wound, trying to clean it, but there was little that could be done to save the situation. Although the woman immediately received doses of antibiotics, after a few days she was diagnosed with a septic infection and a generalized poisoning. We didn't succeed in saving her. The head doctor wrote up the case as an accidental death, because the student was the son of a very good friend of his, a high-ranking official. Before me unfolded the great scientific road to Leningrad. That night I created a chilling scene for my family at home. I swallowed sedatives with my vodka, then locked myself in the bathroom and howled.

Here, in the quiet countryside, I had a strange dream many times over. I was standing in an empty field. Two women approached me. I recognized them: one was Serafima, the other was the dead woman. Serafima came to me and said that she was not alive. The dead woman said she was the one who was alive. I stood there, confused, not knowing what to say. The alive one was dead, the dead one, alive. I woke drenched in sweat.

It was early morning. My daughter was quietly setting out dishes. She was getting ready for school. I smelled the delicious aroma of coffee. She was brewing it for me. It had been no more than a bad dream. The pain in my breast subsided.

*

As was our custom, I brought a large mug of coffee into my mother's room, without sugar or milk.

'I had a dreadful dream last night,' she said. We weren't accustomed to recounting our dreams to each other. Dreams were dreams; reality was reality.

The reality was this: we were alive. Mundane things shaped our days, the days became weeks, the weeks, months, the months, a year. They stuck together very much like the lumps of clay in our ceramics workshop, which I attended twice a week at the community centre. The fresh clay stood there in large blocks, wrapped in cellophane. It reminded me of the large block of butter that the storekeeper cut into small pieces with a wire much like the one that cut the clay. Our instructor was a sculptor who came from the city and, like my mother, always smelled of cigarettes and alcohol. As the workshop began, she would distribute wire-cut lumps of clay. She showed us various techniques: for example, how to fashion a clay box from a paper pattern. Yet we were free to knead and shape the clay as we saw fit. Follow your instincts, the instructor used to say, pulling her knobbly beret over one eye, wrapped in a piece of clothing she called a poncho and lighting up her next cigarette with relish. We followed her instructions.

In the beginning the clay was tough to knead. It resisted my fingers. Gradually it warmed, then became soft and malleable. I already had a couple of clay dishes with scalloped edges at home, also a squirrel and two medals with the inscription 'Greetings on 8 March', surrounded by appliquéd, colourfully glazed flowers. These were intended as a surprise for my mother and grandmother on International Women's Day. But today I wanted to make something special.

In my mind's eye, I saw my mother's drawing. It was a vague memory. I tried to recall how the foetus looked inside a womb. Very like a large bean, yet with discernible human features. Somewhat curled up, drawn into itself. It wasn't easy to shape. At first my foetus was just an indistinct mass. I kneaded it with my fingers, rolling it on the table, now stretching it, now compressing it. Seeing my confusion, the instructor asked me what I was trying to create. A baby still in her mother's womb, I replied. She extinguished her cigarette and helped me to create a smooth, curved shape. 'You don't have to make a precise image,' she said. But I wanted to create it exactly as my mother's precise drawing appeared in my memory. Now the head was turning out too big, and the arms and legs were too spindly and small.

Angered at my helplessness, I punched the clumsy baby into a lump again and tried anew. Everyone else was shaping the usual charming dishes and animals. Once more I kneaded out a smooth ball, rolled it on the table and made a lovely curved shape, much as the instructor had done previously. I was afraid to handle it further, afraid to blunder again and find another clumsy baby in my hands. I gazed at the smooth, mute shape. Would I be able to breathe life into it? The instructor was already coming to inspect our work and to correct what we had done. I didn't have the courage to touch my curved shape any more.

I stood there with my hands tightly fisted. I could do nothing for myself, nothing for the clay baby, who lay on the table unborn. Frustrated, I decided to destroy it altogether. I stamped my fist into the curved shape. The instructor came over and said, 'I see you've managed to do it.' I gazed at the three-part chrysalis. The outline of a tiny human being was clearly discernible. It wasn't as precise as my mother's drawing, but it was there. I gave it to my mother. I think she hid it somewhere. At least I never noticed it anywhere at home after that.

I was sorry that my mother had hidden the clay baby. I thought of it as a magic baby because that evening, coming home from the ceramics workshop, I felt an odd, new pain in my groin. Suddenly I needed to pee. I knelt behind a bush, pulled down my knickers and noticed a streak of blood in them. I wasn't afraid; my mother had told me that this would happen one day and that afterwards it would happen every month.

I told my mother that I was menstruating much later. It came with great pain and made me faint a couple of times in school. The clay baby had brought new times.

*

My daily walk to the ambulatory centre led past our village's Lutheran church, which housed a book archive. This church had been lucky: elsewhere churches had been either demolished or reappointed to suit the needs of the *kolkhoz* – they became storehouses for fertilizers and animal feed. My parents never talked about God. No one talked about Him because it had been clearly announced: He didn't exist. I had just one childhood story for a proof of His existence.

Once my grandmother came to visit us and I was left in her care for the evening. She was making a *buberts* – a sweet concoction of beaten egg, cream of wheat and milk floating in cranberry sauce. While she cooked, she described how, as a child, bundled in blankets and furs, she had been made to sit out in a sleigh on a cold winter night. The small bells fixed to the harness had tinkled and the horse had drawn the sleigh to church. There, still wrapped in blankets, she had been carried into the church. While the minister was preaching, she had seen a man dressed in light, summer clothes in the dark outside the church window. Surely He had been God. Later he had been seen lying in a ditch, under a church window frame with its pane intact. No one had had the courage to go near him to see if he was alive or dead.

I still haven't had the opportunity to meet Him. That's what I in my student naiveté had said to the old professor, who, of course, reported my ambiguous comment to his superiors. As I had responded to my Engels Street interrogator, I didn't believe in God. But I thought about Him more and more frequently. About whether God was or wasn't there when Serafima and my other patients became pregnant, lying on this outdated examination chair made of cracked fake leather, their legs in stirrups of cold, uncomfortable metal. No one and nothing gave me the slightest sign that He was there. How could I feel anything of His existence? Everything or almost everything could be explained without His presence.

She came by chance. It was evening and consulting hours were nearly finished. A quiet knock at my door. 'Come in,' I said. She looked very much like Serafima – her head was wrapped in a large shawl and she didn't speak Latvian. She sat down shyly on the couch. For many months now she had suffered back and lower stomach pains. She had tried not only teas but also ointments and prayers – nothing had helped. She no longer had the strength to tolerate the pain.

Still in her shawl, she clambered onto the examination chair. I asked her to remove her vest and blouse and to raise her brassiere. Over her breasts she clasped her cross – like the one that Serafima wore – and allowed herself to be examined.

I had only to see her nipples and all was clear. They had drawn inward. Her right breast and her underarm region were full of lumps. She hadn't seen a female doctor for almost fifteen years.

'You have to go to the city right away for more detailed tests. These will doubtless be followed by an operation,' I said.

'Is it cancer?' she asked.

'Most likely it is, but it could be something else,' I answered. 'The sooner you get to a hospital, the better.'

'I've never been in a hospital,' she said as she got dressed. It was impossible to tell her age. Her face naive and childlike, her skin smooth, her hands work-worn and deeply veined.

'Maybe I'll still try with prayers,' she said.

'I very strongly recommend you don't drag this out but go straight to a hospital,' I said in a strict voice.

'Doctor, do you believe in God?' she asked.

'I still haven't had the opportunity to meet Him,' I repeated. An odd sensation gripped my stomach.

'What a pity. It's one of the most beautiful meetings in life. Love and fidelity for a lifetime. A friend who always supports and forgives you.'

What she said seemed to me naive and exaggerated. Through my clairvoyant eyes I saw her cancer-riddled body, which, most likely, could no longer be helped either by an operation or by God.

'Come,' she said. 'Through the woods, on a hill above the river, is a small Orthodox church. There are no windows, it's boarded up, but you can pray quietly there. No one goes there. It's safe.'

I had never heard of this small church.

'Come on Sunday morning. I'll read a prayer.'

It was an empty Sunday without my daughter. It had snowed heavily and the walk through the woods was not easy. We never walked in that direction. A path trampled by animals led along the edge of the forest. It gradually narrowed to no more than a snow-covered trail. On the other side of the trail nestled a river in its winter sleep. It seemed incredible that a church could be here. Soon its silhouette rose through the trees. Two small, round

cupolas. Effectively there were no windows, as they'd
been boarded up. The door was half-open. In the darkness inside, lit by flames from tapers, a subdued voice
was chanting. A candlelit icon was propped up high on
the dilapidated altar: the Mother of God, with a halo of
light around her head and a child in her arms. A woman
stood facing the icon and chanting from a small book.
I didn't understand the words. They washed over me
like a wave:

*О, Пресвятая и Преблагословенная Мати
Сладчайшаго Господа нашего Иисуса Христа!
Припадаем и поклоняемся Тебе пред святою и
пречестною иконою Твоею, еюже дивны и прес-
лавны чудеса содеваеши, от огненнаго запаления
и молниеноснаго громе жилища наша спасавши,
недужныя исцеляеши и всякое благое прошение
наше во благо исполняеши. Смиренно молим Тя,
всесильная рода нашего Заступнице, сподоби ны
немощныя и грешныя Твоего Матерняго участия
и благопопечения...*

Then something slipped into place. I did understand:

O most holy Virgin Mary, I praise thy mercy and I
pray to thee: purify my mind, teach me to walk the
straight path set by Christ's commandments. Grant
me strength, so I may awake, sing and banish heavy-
hearted sleep. In your prayers, Bride of God, deliver

me who am fettered by sin. Protect me night and day, save me from my enemies, who war against me. Giver of Life, Mother of Christ, grant a new life to me, whom earthly passions have vanquished. Thou, who hast given birth to the never-waning Light, light my darkened soul. Heavenly Father, our Redeemer, make me the dwelling of the Divine Spirit. Thou, who hast given birth to the Healer, heal my soul of yearning and sinful passions. Tossed in life's storms, lead me to the port of penitence. Save me from eternal fire, the evil worm and hell.

*

It was almost summer. Over the past winter something had changed. My mother appeared calm and balanced. My persistent fear had abated. On several evenings my mother had supper prepared for me. In free moments, we would read together or work in the garden. We raked leaves and fallen branches under which energetic green shoots were edging upwards. It was the loveliest time in our small garden. Soon everything would be in blossom. The old trees were still vigorous. The apple trees blossomed every second year or so, but the cherry trees and the pear still every year. Later into full summer, the roses would add their perfume, then the jasmine.

One more year and our life would have to change. The nearest secondary school, where I was to continue my schooling, was far away. I wouldn't be able to walk to and from classes. I would have to move and board during the week.

On the day we received our report cards my mother came home from work on time. She had managed to get a couple of éclairs and some cream-filled *trubochka*. I brewed tea. In the garden under the old cherry tree, we set out a small table and two chairs. Coolness still rose from the ground, but the air was fragrant and warm. My mother smiled when I opened my report card. There was only one 4 there – for physical education. The rest were 5s – the highest mark possible. She patted my head. I leaned down and kissed her cheek.

We knew that we wouldn't see each other for at least two months. My grandmother and step-grandfather were taking me on a holiday to the Black Sea. We had to take a train for several days to Simferopol, and from there still further to Alushtai, which was right on the seashore.

I was sorry my mother had to remain on her own.

'But don't you worry,' I said. 'I'll return in time to go mushrooming.'

'I'll be fine,' my mother said. 'Get some sun, swim and eat a lot of fruit.'

The May evening embraced us.

'Mamma,' I said, and was frightened, for I had never addressed my mother like that. 'Mamma, after the eighth grade I would like to go back to my grandparents in the city. There's a secondary school very close by our flat, you know.'

There it was, out in the open. A great stone rolled off my chest.

My mother took out a cigarette packet. She lit a match, then a cigarette.

'Probably that's the right thing to do,' she said. She looked so sad and vulnerable that a lump formed in my throat.

'I'll come and visit you often, and we still have a whole year ahead of us.' I was talking for the sake of talking.

'It'll be fine,' she said in a quiet voice. 'But eat your éclair or the cream pastry. You've more than earned it. You're like me in my dream,' she said. 'Outdoors, in the middle of a circle, where you're being pulled on both sides, and it hurts.'

I didn't understand this dream. But yes, each time these partings hurt. I tried to get accustomed to the pain and to be joyful about the reunion that came with each changeover from mother to grandparents and back.

The train that raced towards the south took me away from the pain. Our compartment was clean and comfortable. The attendant brought tea for us. My grandmother had prepared tasty treats for the trip, while two evenings in a row my step-grandfather took us to the dining car. There you could get not only chicken Kiev but also stroganoff and *shashlik* and *kupaty* sausages. My grandmother and step-grandfather each had a glass of cognac while I had Tarhun, a fizzy drink. Ukraine's small railway stations soon replaced the Belarusian forests. At these stations we spotted old ladies in kerchiefs and men selling pears and apricots in pails. We were nearing paradise.

At Simferopol station my step-grandfather rented a white Zhiguli car and driver to take us to Alushtai. We drove with the windows rolled down, and a warm southern wind tousled our hair. It was another world. I hadn't thought of my mother at any point on the journey. She had disappeared as if wound up in a ball of yarn that rolled away into the distance.

That warm evening at the end of our long journey, our landlady treated us to a juicy watermelon. Behind our table was an arbour overgrown with grapevines, from which clusters of unripe grapes as good as fell into our mouths. I asked permission to pluck some. The landlady laughed and encouraged me to look for ripe ones. Bushes and trees I had never seen grew in her garden, unfamiliar fruit ripening in their branches.

In the morning, after a light breakfast, the three of us walked to the sea. My grandmother was wearing a white linen dress, my step-grandfather a short-sleeved shirt and wide, flapping trousers. My grandmother had bought a swimsuit for me – a two-piece, orange with a pattern of fishes. I was hopping about like a colt in an excess of joy.

There it was. Enormous, endless, glistening in the morning sun. The foaming waves caressed the shore, playing a tambourine on the pebbles. Mirrored in the bright bluish-green water was the clean, clear sky. Not a cloud could be seen as far as the horizon. We stood on the shore, spellbound.

'Let's run, Sweet Pea, let's run,' my grandmother suddenly exclaimed, throwing off her dress and sandals.

I tore off my dress and we ran. The foaming salty water enveloped us.

'As warm as milk,' my grandmother said.

I swam up to her and hugged her tightly. For a brief while, hanging onto each other and swaying in the waves, I felt my mother's spirit join us. We three were bound so closely. My step-grandfather stood on the shore, waving cheerfully.

One evening, as my grandmother and step-grandfather sat with our landlady over a glass of wine, I asked permission to go by myself as far as the sea.

'Just don't go into the water,' cautioned my step-grandfather.

The beach was already almost empty of holiday-makers. In the dark sky of this southern summer just a few stars shone. The sea was calm, the water lapping lazily against the pebbles, filling the air with a sound like the tinkling of crotal bells.

I thought about my mother and her overheated room at the ambulatory centre. About the endless line of women in the corridor. About her equally overheated room at home. About her daily mugs of coffee and her cigarettes. About the books, the only thing in which she found comfort. And I thought about this endless land, sea and sky, of which even a fingernail's worth of dirt was denied her. About the grapes, which she would never pluck from an arbour over her head. About the sound of the crotal bells, which she would not hear, and about the love-filled air, which she would not breathe.

I waded into the water up to my ankles. She wasn't here, yet she was here.

*

The river was warm as milk. Only late at night could it provide relief from the sweltering heat. The days felt interminable; the short nights brought the balm of darkness. At the end of July the ambulatory centre was closed for a month. I began a long, lonely, senseless time. I lay naked in my shadow-filled room, trying to kill the nights and days.

I couldn't read. Letters followed one another forming sentences, sliding past my eyes, my thoughts, which lingered elsewhere. Now and then I thought of my daughter, my mother and stepfather. I tried to envisage their happy threesome on the southern seashore. Paradise was there and it lacked for nothing. Now and then I thought of hell and of the Giver of Life – although I had not seen that patient again. I walked to the church a couple of times more, but it was empty and silent.

The Giver of Life. A powerful title, against which the words 'hell' and 'evil worm' sounded trivial and insignificant. Still, those words were devouring me.

We Soviet doctors all swore an oath to fight for life and health. We swore to avert the threat of nuclear war and to serve our Soviet people and our motherland. *Prisyaga, vracha Sovetskogo Soyuza* – the Doctor's Oath of the Soviet Union. The evil worm had eroded the Hippocratic oath, in which, calling on all the gods as witnesses, the young healer promised not to give any woman any substance or means that could result in foeticide, or to turn from virtue and piety either in her life or in her professional duties. And we solemnly swore: if I fulfil and don't transgress this oath, may I be successful both in my life and in the art of my profession. But if I break this oath or swear falsely, may the opposite come to pass.

The opposite had happened. And I was trapped in the white heat of the inferno.

At last the balmy evening drew me outside. The late jasmine was savagely fragrant. The dog had dug a cool den at its roots. I took a towel, locked the gate and headed for the river. It was worth suffering the day for the sake of this evening walk.

The track led down over the steep, clay bank from which seeped fresh rivulets of water. These fed into the river, mingling with its dark waters and becoming one great flow. The current was deceptive at this point. It suddenly made a turn and could carry you away from the bank. You had to gather every ounce of strength to swim against it.

The fragrance of meadow flowers wafted along the riverbank. The aroma of wild mint blended with meadowsweet and sweet flag.

I sat on a large rock that still retained the day's sweltering heat. I lit a cigarette. The river was calm, hiding her currents deep down. Mist rose against the pallid light where the sun was setting. The long, senseless day wrestled with a redeeming night.

An aeroplane roared by in the dark sky, prompting both fear and longing. I remembered myself quite young, dressed up, holding my mother's hand. We were walking down a street when a plane flew overhead and my mother flinched, grabbed me and ran into a courtyard. Then she calmed down and we continued on our way in the city streets. I'd been gripped with a new fear, but also a longing for the distant place that plane was speeding to.

Now at the riverbank, with one day ending and the promise of another, and another beyond that, I felt the same. Like my cigarettes smoked down to ashes, life's end drew nearer.

I took off my clothes and slipped into the warm river. The river of life – it would absolve me of my sin. It would forgive me for ending the life of a foetus and for undermining the parenthood I had sworn to uphold. May the opposite come to pass.

*

I returned to my mother's house at the end of August. Behind me was the miraculous summer at the southern sea. The sun had bleached my hair and I was tanned. 'You're shaping up to be beautiful,' my mother said. My mother, our small dwelling, the garden, the dog – all looked different to me now. Petty and shrunken, grey and dust-covered, but still dear.

'The summer has been hot. The one saving grace was evenings at the river,' my mother told me. She examined my gifts: a big yellow quince, seashells, some colourful bits of glass worn smooth by the sea and edible chestnuts. 'Remember,' I said, 'you bought some like these in the Riga market, when you asked me to live with you. I wanted to remind you of their taste.'

Her gaze spoke of utter defeat. Just a bit longer and I would be leaving. I was still swimming in an enormous, clear blue sea, where the waves played their tambourine against the pebbles and promised a wondrous future.

One morning my mother woke me while it was still dark. 'Get up and dress warmly,' she said, laying a raincoat and rubber boots beside my bed. My heart leapt in excitement. We were going mushrooming. Lately I hadn't been able to convince my mother to go to the woods. Usually I went on my own and stayed close to the forest's edge because I was afraid of getting lost. But now as a pair we'd be able to criss-cross the forest to our hearts' content. Following close on the heels of the heatwave, the August squalls were the right time for mushrooms. We were united in our conspiracy. We would go wherever the forest paths led: whatever it took to attain a full basket of king boletes.

The day was just dawning as we made our way into the forest. The sky was overcast. A warm mist lay in the meadow. A solitary bird was jabbering away. He dragged his beak along a tree trunk, announcing his presence. My

mother and I padded on into the forest, where a mushroom kingdom awaited us. The overcast sky slid open a
crack and a feeble sunbeam crept out, then grew stronger.
Soon golden light flooded the forest. Dew trembled in
spurs of fir, pine, birch and aspen trees and ferns. The
spider's webs sparkled.

We walked in silence, concentrating. Talking could
scare them. Beneath ferns, among aspen trees, squatted scaber stalks with chubby stems and deep red caps.
Further on, a thick blanket of black leaves concealed
ugly green milk caps. Then at intervals along the forest
path giant boletes exploded from the soil, surrounded by
small slippery jacks, clusters of chanterelles and orange
milk caps. Gypsy mushrooms and copper brittle gill but-
tons lay cradled in the moss. We maintained our silence,
though we felt like yelling for joy. My mother's glasses
began to steam up. Eventually she tore them off and put
them in her pocket. In a meadow beyond the forest we
found white horse mushrooms. These were large, powerful balls lifted by strong stalks, veiled by floating skirts.
Our baskets were filling up.

We sat down in the sun at the forest's edge to catch
our breath and rest for a moment. My mother unwrapped
some sandwiches. The fragrance of moss beneath us, of
the mushrooms in our baskets and the bark behind us,
was golden as the sky.

'I don't remember how you taught me to differentiate
between them,' I said to my mother.

'Between the safe mushrooms and the deadly ones?'

'Yes,' I said, 'how to tell the edible from the poisonous. I don't remember how that happened.'

'We went together. I described and pointed them out to you. I also don't remember exactly.'

'Now I simply know. I walk, pick and know.'

'Don't be so confident. You still have to be careful.'

'If I don't know I don't pick the mushroom.'

'But how do you know that you don't know?' my mother asked.

'I don't know how, I simply know. I know that from you.'

Having finished our sandwiches, we were silent once more. We crossed the meadow to reach a stand of lime trees. Their leaves had already started to yellow. Dried blossoms were drifting from the oldest trees. There weren't supposed to be mushrooms here. Yet through the leaves on the ground peeked red stalks with grey caps. Their shapes were like the boletes, but their colours were new. Beneath each cap was a strange yellow-gilled sponge. I didn't recognize these mushrooms. My mother examined them with acute interest.

'Do you know these?' I asked.

'I don't know,' she said, starting to cut the mushrooms and to put them in the basket.

'Why are you cutting them, then?'

'I'll have to check them out,' my mother answered.

On our way back, the sun disappeared and a light rain began to fall. Exhausted, rain-soaked, with full baskets, we returned home.

I was convinced that once my mother looked over the mushrooms found in the lime tree copse, she'd throw them on the compost. But she cleaned them carefully and made a separate pile for them. I felt a pinch of the old fear.

'Mamma, you aren't going to try those mushrooms on yourself, are you?' I spoke up when the pots on the wood stove were already bubbling and the pans were sizzling.

'There are only two possibilities: either they're safe or they're deadly,' my mother said. I noticed an odd kind of fascination in her eyes.

'Are you not afraid you'll die?' I asked in despair.

'No, I'm not afraid. But we don't know if death is certain from them,' my mother snapped back, continuing to clean the boletes, chanterelles and orange milk caps.

I wanted to grab those damn colourful pretend-boletes and throw them on the fire.

But my mother boiled them. She tasted them that very evening.

'See, they turned out to be safe mushrooms after all,' she said calmly, when I brought up her big mug of morning coffee.

I sat down on my mother's bed and looked on as she lit her first cigarette. I thought about what had really happened. Was she playing with life and death? Was she the most courageous woman in the world, who wanted to know what she didn't know? I reached for her blanket-covered legs and pressed my face against them. Thus we sat there for a moment.

*

The usual hamster's wheel of the ambulatory centre began again. The hot summer had done its work. They came and came, mainly wanting to get rid of their foetuses. I thanked my exile for ridding me of the means to do this for them. I just confirmed that they were pregnant. I didn't try to tell them how the tiny foetus can evade the instrument attempting to scrape it out of the mother's womb. Or that this is effected knowingly by both of us, my patient and me. Or that the man often knows nothing and prefers to know nothing about it, for these are women's concerns in a woman's world.

I often thought of the woman who'd been chanting in the church. Finally she came to see me. As I had anticipated, her right breast had been removed. But she radiated determination and vitality. The doctor in the city had told her that for the time being she had no reason to worry. The malignancy had been cut out and she was free of it for now.

I told her that I had gone up to the church several times but had found it empty.

Well yes, no one except her ever went there. But now she would go again and more often. Because she had to thank the Giver of Life, for the malignancy had been stopped. The one who had given birth to the Healer had healed her.

She left me a tiny picture: the same icon to which she had been chanting. And she gave me a slim wax taper to light when I felt sad.

On the point of leaving, she turned around and asked how I had been able to diagnose her malady.

'That's just from experience,' I said. 'Medical experience.'

'No, no,' she said. 'I see that you can see more clearly.' She said goodbye and left.

I opened the window to air the room. The September wind whipped up a maelstrom of yellow leaves which flew into the room, scattering the papers on my desk. The picture of the Virgin had fallen face down. '*Pokhozha na vas*' – 'Just like you' – was written on the back.

*

As always, the school year began during the beetroot and carrot harvest. The autumn squalls did not let up. Drenched, we squatted on our boxes, cutting off beetroot tops and twisting off carrot tops. The piles in the field appeared interminable. I swore to do everything possible so that I would never, ever again have to sit rain-soaked on a box, wearing freezing mud-caked gloves and cutting off beetroot tops. A year from now I would join the Young Communist League. Then it would be summer and I would move back to the city and enrol in a secondary school. It would be the start of a new era.

The work in the *kolkhoz* fields dragged on. Our classes, therefore, only started in October. Having gone from the wet fields into the bright, warm classrooms, we needed at least a week to get back into the rhythm of school. Our *kurtkas*, pullovers and rubber boots were replaced by school uniforms. Instead of eating in the field kitchen, where tea, bread and great vats of stew had been brought to us and consumed with relish on the spot, lunch was now in the school lunch room.

'It's good that you won't have to slave any more,' my mother said one evening. 'Everything will be different in the city school.'

I sensed the pain of parting in her voice. The pain that for all these years I'd got to know in my very bones. The years of exile had brought us closer.

At school we were rehearsing Anna Sakse's *Pasakas par ziediem* – 'Fairy Tales about Flowers'. I was given the part of a jasmine plant. In the evening my mother and I role-played the fairy tale's ending. She was the artist who loved painting in many different colours and who wanted to be begged by the jasmine to give it colour, and I was the jasmine who refused to bend or to beg.

'It's a beautiful fairy tale,' my mother said. 'Life often makes one bend.'

But I had fully entered my jasmine character. I wouldn't bend and I wouldn't beg. Even if my face was splashed with paint, I would stand straight or I would break. And I played my role very well. In a white costume made from an old sheet, on the steps of the small stage in the school music room, I stood unshakeable, even when the artist spattered me with yellow paint. A splash of paint even caught me in the face. People laughed. But I stood stiff as a post, looking straight in the faces of everyone laughing, until they fell silent. The narrator's voice rang in the silence: 'Try to bend her – she'll break.'

Soon life dragged us from a fairy tale into ghastly reality. Brezhnev died on 10 November. Everyone had thought that he was immortal but he died. The school hung a large picture of him draped with a black mourning ribbon in the gymnasium. What would happen next? We were convinced that war would break out.

The day of Brezhnev's funeral, our school was given a holiday, on the condition that we watched the funeral on television.

This seemed like idiocy to my mother. She had bought two bottles of wine and was drinking in her room. Still afraid that war was imminent, I settled down in the front room. I turned on our television and saw how the army and statesmen had gathered at the Kremlin in Moscow. They were playing a funeral dirge. The most awful thing was that they dropped Brezhnev's casket into the waiting hole with an enormous clatter. No one saw it, but it's very likely, judging from the noise, that he tumbled out of his casket, turned over and fell into his grave on his face. A dreadful thing to imagine.

After Brezhnev's funeral no one felt much like talking. A terrible sense of foreboding hung in the air. My mother drank every evening. Three days after the funeral, on 18 November, she lit candles. She laid three rows of Michaelmas daisies on her table: two of red flowers and between them one of white. Her pupils were dilated and she was talking strangely. I was afraid to be in the same room with her. Now and then I opened the door to her room to see if she was all right.

'Maybe a miracle will happen. Maybe now a miracle will happen,' she mumbled.

'Mamma, be reasonable. What miracle?' I grabbed her shoulders and shook her. 'Now there won't be a miracle but war. Mamma, there's going to be a war, maybe even a nuclear war, and we are all going to die!' I almost screamed. I was afraid of the war and once again afraid of my mother.

'I wish Latvia the best!' She emptied the second bottle of wine. She was thoroughly drunk.

I rolled her into bed, covered her and in despair searched her room and her handbag. I threw all the tablets that I found into the stove.

All night I sat by my mother's bed, now and then feeling her forehead and for her pulse. Sometimes it raced like mad and other times it was feeble, almost imperceptible. Occasionally her heavy breathing was interrupted by a flood of words. My mother was talking in her wine- and drug-induced sleep. About the miracle that would happen, about freedom, about the triple-striped flag that would fly – the red, white and red again, about God, who would bless it, about Latvia, which would live for ever. Then she paused, breathing heavily. Then screamed – 'It's breaking, breaking, breaking.' Then fell silent again.

I lay down beside her and pressed myself close. I was trembling all over. If her pulse had slowed any further, I would have run to the neighbours and called an ambulance.

But gradually her breathing grew calmer and less erratic. Sweat beaded her forehead. I wiped it away. The candles burned out on the table. Their fragrance blended with the aroma of the Michaelmas daisies. I opened the window and the tranquil air of November filled the room.

*

The war did not start. Slowly the quotidian round was smothering me. Soon I would be alone with this daily routine. The autumn would become winter, the winter, spring; spring would turn into summer and then my daughter would leave. Already shrivelling, life's hot-air balloon would deflate even more. And *my* life, slinking from home to the ambulatory centre, from the ambulatory centre back home like a whipped dog, would shrink away too.

I had to work harder to manage my patients. The impression that I was seeing through them grew stronger. With one glance I could tell what was ailing them. Almost all my diagnoses turned out to be correct. My patients returned again and again to their miracle doctor.

Then my powers to perform miracles were put to the test. One morning, walking down the corridor with its waiting women, I noticed her immediately. Although there were no free seats left except beside her, no woman had chosen to sit there. They were keeping their distance. Her face attracted attention instantly: it was neither a woman's nor a man's. As did her hands – she had taken off her gloves and crossed her hands in her lap. The palms were enormous, the fingers, powerful. These were not a woman's hands.

When she timidly entered my consulting room I was surprised by how diminutive she was. Surely that's why her palms looked so enormous. I asked her to describe all her ailments and to undress for examination.

'Will you really examine me?' she asked in disbelief, the timbre of her voice low and husky. 'In several places doctors have refused to do so. But I need to know what I am,' she said, and tears sprang to her eyes.

'Calm down,' I said, handing her a glass of water. 'Everything will be fine. What's your name?'

'I've an odd name,' she said. 'Jesse. It was given me by my foster mother in the orphanage. I've always struggled with this name, although I work as a charwoman.'

I washed my hands and looked on as she slowly unwrapped her heavy clothes. It seems I had inspired her trust, for she continued to tell me about herself.

'When I grew older, my orphanage mother showed me a piece of paper that had been included in my blanket when I was abandoned at the orphanage. Written on it was: "I don't want this gift." She told me that Jesse means "a gift".'

Undressed, she was very uncomfortable. She tried to hide her private parts with her large hands. She stood before me, one of God's bitter jokes. A small man's body with a woman's crotch. In the place of breasts not even the tiniest of buds – it was a man's chest.

I did my examination.

Dressed once more, she gazed at me with gratitude.

I plucked up my courage and said, 'Externally you're partly a woman, but internally you're partly a man.'

She looked at me as if she had been informed of a malignant ailment or infertility. Then she broke into tears. Through her sobs she repeated, 'No, I am a woman, I am a woman, I am a woman...' Finally, calming down a little, she asked, 'Can that man not be cut out of me?'

'That can't be done. Something else could be tried, but unfortunately I don't have the ability to help you.'

'Thanks for not turning me away,' Jesse said as she closed my consulting-room door.

I sat there, as much a fool as Jesse. My exile had bound my hands. I couldn't compete with God, although just then I wished to more than anything. The Leningrad Institute was unreachable, but it was there that new discoveries were being made in hormone therapy. Only this might provide Jesse with a path to a happy life as a woman. She would never be pregnant and carry a child, but she might experience the growth of breasts or some other feminine miracle.

Everything comes full circle. The snow-covered bridge over the River Neva and my naive question to the drunkard at the God's Ear café: 'Is Jesse only a man's name?'

My head was fit to burst. This damned cage, in which I could do nothing. I opened the window. There she went – Jesse, God's gift, whom I couldn't help. Suddenly she turned, took off one glove, waved farewell and raised two fingers in a victory sign.

*

The war did not start and life moved on in its accustomed tracks. I turned fourteen. Now I could join the Young Communist League. I had to learn the statutes. Our literature teacher said I could recite, for example, Ojārs Vācietis's poem 'Noraisot kaklautu' – 'Taking off My Neckerchief' – to mark the poet's death in November. I took several of his collections out of the library. It was strange how one man could write such diverse poems. I liked this one: 'Man ir smeldzīga, smeldzīga nojauta, ka tā pasaule, kurā es dzīvoju, var daudz ātrāk par tavu būt nojaukta' – 'I have a painful, painful intuition that the world, where I live, can be demolished much sooner than yours.' But that would not appeal to the Komsomol, so I obeyed the teacher and was rewarded with my Communist Youth badge and membership card.

This year winter seemed short. Already in February it was warm and sunny. We waited for spring and rehearsed our songs for the 8 March concert. My heart was filled with an unusual joy. Though its light was still wintry, the sun was melting snow drifts and icicles. Birds silenced by winter could now be heard singing. Everything was moving towards a thaw, towards spring. Then the holidays would come, then the final school term, and primary school would be finished. And my first summer without rows of beetroot, cucumbers and carrots would begin, after which would follow an autumn in the city – at a new school with new school friends.

My mother now came into my room quite frequently. Or I would wander into hers. We ate our supper. We curled up in bed, sometimes in silence, at other times exchanging a few words. The dog went from room to room with us, not wanting to be left alone.

'I'll have to learn to live differently,' she said to me one evening. 'I've become used to you.'

'Me too.' We had our small, isolated life. Somewhere was another life, but we had ours.

My mother often left a light burning all night in her room. If I didn't fall asleep right away, I would hear her going to the kitchen to brew coffee and going back again. Sometimes it seemed to me she didn't sleep at all. All around her bed encyclopedias and other books were scattered. And sketches, which for the most part I didn't understand. I recognized medical instruments in some of them, and in others, a woman's crotch. They were frightening. I didn't tell my mother about my first gynaecological examination at school. It was painful and repulsive. Of course, I thought about my mother, about her daily work at the ambulatory centre. I didn't understand why she'd chosen such work. A small inner voice taunted me: 'Guess, guess this little riddle.' But racking my brain got me nowhere.

One night I saw that my mother was asleep with the light still burning in her room. I took out the coffee mugs, collected the apple cores and bread crusts. Apples and black rye bread were my mother's favourite food. I turned out the light. The window was half-open. She kept it like that, to let some air into the smoke-filled room. Fresh, fragrant night air flowed in. Moonlight illuminated us.

My mother was sleeping on her left, her face turned to the window. She slept calmly. I sat across from her on a small stool. Her face was covered with freckles, like mine. In the winter they had faded somewhat, but were still visible. She had a high forehead on which tiny wrinkles were slowly forming. Once in a while she used to place her hand on my forehead and say, 'Never look surprised; never frown.' But she herself frowned often. Her nose was fine and narrow, with a small hump. Her eyebrows and lashes were dark brown, her ears small and close to her head, with small lobes. Now and then she opened her mouth and quietly snored for a while in her sleep. My mother's face looked almost beautiful. Fear, so often another occupant of this room, had disappeared. There was just silence, the fresh night air and the moonlight. And my mother's face.

I sat for a brief while, then left for my own bed. It was hard to fall asleep. I went straight into a dream. I was standing by my old wardrobe. The large oval mirror should have shown me full-length, but I could only see half of me. My hands were crossed over my chest. At first I seemed to see my grandmother. I had her face – her prominent cheekbones, humped nose, grey eyes and high forehead. Then the image in the mirror changed and I saw myself as my mother, her eyes closed, asleep. And then I saw myself with a lightly glowing skin as if taken from a greetings card, but nonetheless myself.

In the morning, as usual, I brought a big mug of coffee into my mother's room. She had risen already, sat down before the broken mirror on her bedside table and was brushing her hair.

'Give me the brush. I'll help you,' I said.

My mother often had tangled hair at the back, which she patted down and tied with an elastic band.

'It has to be combed for once,' I said, and began to untangle Mother's hair.

She submitted, lit a cigarette and sipped her coffee.

'I had a lovely dream. I saw myself in the mirror, first as your mother, then as you and then as me. Your eyes were closed and you were sleeping.'

My mother put her cigarette and coffee mug down on the bedside table. She clasped my hands and placed her face in them. Then she kissed them and quietly repeated, 'Be vigilant. Keep your eyes open.'

*

I hadn't seen them for several years. During the spring break my daughter asked if we could finally go to Riga together. Apparently my mother and stepfather thought I no longer wished to see them. They wanted to discuss my daughter's move back to their flat. There were all sorts of reasons to go.

The morning we went to catch the train happened to be warm and sunny, although it was still March. We walked holding hands. As always, I felt as though my daughter was leading me. She was so happy, rushing along, almost dancing. Just as happily the March snow thawed into meltwater and flowed away. Even in shady spots the snowdrifts were shrinking. I felt as if I were setting out on a forgotten road after many years of winter.

In the small, neglected railway station a fire sputtered feebly in a wood stove. An exhausted night-owl was snoozing on a bench. My daughter knocked on the window of the cashier's booth. The cashier slid open the heavy rag curtain and punched out two tickets for us.

'Mamma, come,' my daughter said. 'You get the best feeling if you wait for the train at the end of the platform.'

Only a few passengers were waiting for the Riga train. We headed for the end of the platform. I joined in with my daughter's ritual. Where the platform finished, the tracks disappeared in the distance between the fields on one side and the forest on the other. There in the spring-like morning haze it had to appear: the train that, after all these years, would take me to the city from which I'd been banished. It would take me to my mother and stepfather, whom I had hurt so much.

In the distance the train roared. It was approaching to take us away from this Golgotha.

The journey was long. Lonely stations slid by the window, followed by the Rumbula Forest corridors, where Jews had been shot. I daydreamed back to a student party in one of the Rumbula's community gardens. Having downed our strong, sour gut-rot, I was looking for somewhere to sit down. The allotment garden was surrounded by a temporary fence supported by posts. Small for its role, covered in moss, each post had a cross scored into it at the top. Cabbages, beetroot and potatoes to provide for our Soviet pigs would grow abundantly here, for bodies from military executions fertilized the soil.

The journey was slow. The train rolled into Šķirotava railway station, from where tens of thousands of Latvians were deported to Siberia. Nothing had changed since that day when my daughter and I had gone into our remote country exile. People were living in the same world, with identical sectional wall units, crockery sets and coffee tables, in identical flats, with identical doormats. They were irreproachable. For in Šķirotava – which means 'place of separation' in Latvian – no one was separated any longer. Husbands were not separated from wives, nor children separated from parents, nor grandparents from grandchildren. No longer separated to become slaves of the twentieth century, to fertilize the vast earth of the motherland.

I also thought about my father, from whom we had been separated right here.

The journey was long. I observed my daughter. Her happy girlish face, her chin pressed against the carriage window.

We got out at Riga station.

'Let's walk, Mamma. Let's not take the tram,' my daughter suggested. 'The weather is so nice and you haven't been here for years. Riga is lovely.'

Yes, the March sun was making it lovely, even though the streets were wet, full of mud and slush.

We decided to sit on a bench in Vērmanis Park. I lit a cigarette. My daughter ate an ice cream.

The passers-by seemed to be dressed for a special occasion. The bright colours and the sun were dazzling.

'Let's go further along Kirova Street,' my daughter said.

'Kirov married Elizabete,' I said, laughing. 'Before, this street used to be called "Elizabete".'

'Fine, Mamma. Along Elizabete to Valdemāra Street, who has now married Gorky. How all the streets have been renamed!' my daughter remarked happily.

'Aren't you too smart for a fifteen-year-old?' Her joy warmed my heart.

On a corner we went into a chocolate shop to buy a treat for ourselves. On the shelf were rows of marzipan figurines called *Dārgais* – 'Dear One'.

'Can we afford a marzipan owl?' my daughter asked me quietly.

'Today we can afford everything. Even a marzipan owl.'

We walked hand in hand. My daughter's contentment was tangible.

'Amptmanis Briedītis married Zaube, Nītaure remained an old maid, but Mičurins married Tompsonu.' She was counting the streets and calling out their 'married' names, the new ones, and the original names.

Nothing had changed in our short street. The new technical school, the library for the visually impaired, the peacetime apartment blocks on one side, the kindergarten on the other side.

At the flat my mother and stepfather welcomed us.

We embraced, and I saw their eyes fill with tears. While the table was being laid, I went into my room. It was sunny and clean, my books lined up neatly on a shelf, on the table a vase of tulips, my daughter's books and keepsakes, the bed covered with my mother's fringed, embroidered blanket. Soon my daughter would be living here.

Lunch passed quietly. My daughter talked about school and her achievements in chemistry and literature. My mother and stepfather now and then cast affectionate looks my way. I sat at the beautifully laid table. They all loved me, but I wasn't there.

After lunch I went out for a walk. My familiar walk to the hospital. Ambulances sped by. Someone was being driven to safety. To be saved, to be kept alive – in this city, in this cage. Because life mattered more than anything.

I decided to stop halfway, at the small park where my mother used to take me to the swings in my childhood. The fragrance of hops and chocolate from nearby factories still mingled in the air.

It was early afternoon. The park was full of melting snow and empty of people. On the paths the city's chubby pigeons fluttered about, and sparrows preened their feathers in the sun. The old swings were still there.

I sat on a swing and pushed off from the slush of snow and mud. I swung higher and higher. Above was the blue canopy of the sky. Below the earth's port of remorse. In between, swinging, I breathed fitfully. Through the small hole in the suitcase, where my mother had hidden me to keep me safe.

*

That night my mother didn't come back. She just phoned from the railway station, saying that she was quite all right. She had decided not to stay the night but rather to head back home. I saw how painful that was for my grandparents.

As always during these visits, my grandmother ran a bath for me. It was the most peaceful feeling: to sit in a warm bath, hearing the television from my grandparents' room.

That night they didn't turn on the television. For a while there was silence. I lay in the bath, now and then submerging myself in the water so as not to hear the unusual silence.

After a while my grandmother spoke: 'We've lost her. What will happen to her? What, for God's sake, will happen to her?'

I heard my grandmother start to weep and my step-grandfather try to comfort her.

'The main thing is that everything is all right with our Sweet Pea.'

'Who is to blame?' repeated my grandmother brokenly. 'She grew up surrounded by love. When we returned from Babīte, the windows here were shattered, it was cold, we hadn't anything to eat. I exchanged my African fur coat for dried sugar beet. My jaw grew sore from chewing at those beets. There was nothing else. But they gave me milk to spare in my breasts. She sucked mother's milk until she was three years old. She was a healthy, strong child. What happened to her?'

I sat in the bathtub and my grandmother's weeping reached me there. After a while she opened the door.

'Sweet Pea, do you want me to wash your back?' Her eyes were still red.

She took the worn sea sponge that we had brought from the south, soaped it and gently rubbed my back.

'Like a dulcimer,' she said lovingly. 'You are like a dulcimer.'

I don't remember my mother ever washing my back. We didn't have a bathtub; that was a city pleasure. As was the touch of my grandmother's hand on my back.

I took my favourite photograph album to bed with me. My grandmother had lined up all the albums on the lowest shelf of the bookcase. There was my step-grandfather's youth, and an album of my grandmother's young days, and an album of movie stars and my mother's childhood and teenage album, in which was written in blue ink: 'As you grow, may your spirit grow in clarity.'

The album was thick with padded cloth covers, a gift to my mother on her fifteenth birthday. It was the key to my mother's life before me. She danced through it, a small ballerina in a white tutu, a girl with two braids by a birch tree, in a haystack, a soil-covered girl in a potato field, a swimmer with dripping hair, a folk dancer, her arms outstretched under a banner with Stalin's words: 'We are for peace and keeping peace', an exemplary student in uniform with the first-aid cross on her left arm, a figure taking part in a procession wearing a starched kerchief, helping her stepfather hold the May Day flag.

Then she grew bigger – like me. She had short hair, wore trousers and black sunglasses. She stood by a river, casting a fishing line, but the rod was smudged and it looked like she was casting a black-and-white rainbow across the river. Then she was standing at the far end of a boat by the motor, her arms flung high as if the entire world belonged to her and she was happy, as happy as a person can be in this world. Now the same expression, having clambered onto a large rock. Now wearing a dress which reached to her knees, around her head a wide bandanna and sunglasses. Then the last pictures in the album. Someone had photographed her several times by barbed wire with a sign in two languages – Russian and Latvian: '*Za provolokami ne khodit – smertelno*' and '*Aiz drātēm neiet – nāvējoši*', both meaning, 'Don't go beyond the barbed wire – danger.' But the photo was so full of life: the unbounded, endless seashore, the white sand of the beach, her wind-blown hair and her embroidered dress.

*

The long days and nights of the spring break prepared me for this new life without my daughter. I tried to spend as much time as I could at the ambulatory centre. My patients squeezed me dry and I allowed them to. I muddled their names, forgot them and got lost in the Babel of their diagnoses. When I closed my eyes at night, I was haunted by their genitals. My passion had turned into a pitiful routine, a dead end. I no longer lived along with my patients' hopes and fears. In fact I now reacted with indifference, even to an appalling diagnosis. I simply referred them elsewhere. But they returned: they didn't want any other doctor.

Even Jesse secured a charwoman's job at the ambulatory centre. 'How nice. I'll be working right here near you,' she said, when we ran into each other in the corridor.

Morning and evening, Jesse was a reminder of the cage in which I lived and worked. I had figured out several hormone formulae which might, just possibly, lead Jesse in the direction of womanhood. But it was clear that it would be impossible to apply them in the reality in which both Jesse and I were living. Each of us was bound to care for our own burdens: I for my patients, she for her cleaning. Outside lay freedom: for me to be a scientist and Jesse, even partially, to be a woman. In the meantime we looked after our cages.

Lonely in the evenings without my daughter, after the long workday I invited Jesse to come with me to the river to drink my patients' gifts.

As every spring, the river sloughed its accumulated winter flotsam out onto its banks. Reborn, it flowed slow and fresh, its waters sparkling at the sky.

We sat on a bank.

Our evening by the river was almost silent until we were interrupted by the whirring of wings. A pigeon landed on a driftwood stump nearby. An odd bird, it ducked its head to and fro and stared at us. It wasn't afraid and didn't fly away. Now we were three.

*

After the spring break, time literally flew. For my literature exam I managed to write compositions not only for myself but also for a boy whom I liked. Although he was the shortest, he was also the naughtiest boy at school. He was the most attractive, too, because his face reminded us of a foreign movie star. His father allowed him to drive his coffee-coloured Zhiguli car, he always had money, and once at school he treated me to a banana. It was the first banana I ever ate. It looked as though he liked me.

Now graduation from my primary school was close at hand. My grandmother had managed to find me a white lace blouse, a black skirt with a wide belt and accordion-pleated flounces, and violet-coloured flat shoes, so that I wouldn't be taller than the boy of my choice when we danced.

My mother had almost regained her spirits. She dug out a small crimson bow tie. I thought only boys could wear bow ties, but my mother said that this would make my graduation outfit particularly chic. And she was right. At the graduation neither my male nor my female school friends had bow ties; everyone was talking about it.

My grandmother and my step-grandfather brought gifts and flowers. They sat beside my mother in the hall.

I had the best report card in the school. After the formal ceremony there was some free time before the evening's dancing. My mother invited my grandparents to come back to our house. This was the first time they had visited us.

My step-grandfather walked around the garden, the dog following his every step, because he had been used only to women. I led my grandmother into my room. She sat down at my desk and gazed out of the window. Once more I saw tears fill her eyes.

'Stop, please! It's a celebration today. And in the autumn I'm coming to stay with you.'

My mother had set a table in the garden with simple refreshments. The apple trees were still in blossom. The white blossoms fell on the table and into the lemonade.

'We haven't had a bad life here,' my mother said. 'We'll see how I do on my own.'

My grandmother and my step-grandfather kept quiet.

'What are all these funeral speeches!' I exclaimed, and kissed them, one after the other. It was spring. I might be in love and had high expectations for the evening dance.

In the midst of my happiness, the inscription from my mother's photo album slipped out: 'As you grow, may your spirit grow in clarity.'

My mother gave us a look so full of sadness that I grew ashamed of my coltish joy.

'It's probably time for you to go to the railway station,' she told my grandparents. 'For you too. Keep them company. Then you'll have to go straight to the dance.'

Why did she always make everything so gloomy? On the way to the railway station I burst into tears. How can one keep on not wanting to live? Even on my graduation day not wanting to, probably also the day I was born not wanting to. 'You saved her from the claws of death. How can she repay you like that?' I said to my grandmother and step-grandfather, who walked beside me in silence. My step-grandfather stopped now and then, to catch his breath. My grandmother took his bag.

In the station we hugged.

'You won't die, will you?' I said – just as I had as a child.

'We won't die, Sweet Pea, we won't die.'

That evening I didn't want to see my mother again. I walked as far as the river and back again to the softly lit community hall, where the dancing was beginning.

I had a feeling he would ask me to dance a slow number with him. 'I Just Called to Say I Love You' crooned from the speakers, and the school's naughtiest and most attractive boy was heading diagonally across the hall towards me. In the beginning we danced a bit apart from each other. I placed my hands on his shoulders and he somewhat fearfully put his around my waist. But it was such a good feeling that we moved closer to each other. I tried not to be taller than him. He touched my neck with his nose. The hall's parquet floor disappeared beneath my feet.

In the warm June night we walked to the river. He gathered small flat stones and flipped them across the water. The stones touched the surface of the water several times, flew the next bit of distance, then sank.

At our house he first kissed me on the cheek, then pressed his lips to mine, which I held tightly pinched together. This was my first kiss.

I carefully opened the front door so as not to wake my mother. Her door was open and her room was empty. Through the open window I saw her cigarette glowing faintly in the garden. She was sitting by our festive table, which was still laden with plates and lemonade glasses.

'Mamma, why are you sitting here alone in the dark?' I asked her, stepping out into the garden.

'I'm afraid, my child. I'm afraid,' she whispered.

She had never called me that before. And she had never talked of fear.

My anger with her dissipated into the warm night.

I hugged my mother tightly. 'Mamma, don't be afraid. You just need to want to live, Mamma. You need to want to live and all will be fine. I love you, Mamma.'

*

It was a sun-drenched summer. Although my mother and stepfather had invited my daughter to come with them to the seaside for a month, she decided to stay with me until mid-August. Everything this summer seemed to play a part in our farewells. Our dog died, probably from eating rat poison. We buried him beside Bambi.

I avoided going into my daughter's room, where everything was gradually being packed for her departure. On her desk stood a daily flip calendar: the summer of 1984 was being turned over, page by page.

Jesse became a frequent visitor. She arrived to help, to tidy, to prepare this and that. The ambulatory centre was closed for a month, so Jesse, who was working part-time in the book archives at the church, slipped me a few things to read, to shorten my long, sleepless nights.

Jesse also told me about books whose covers were torn, so as to obscure their authors and titles, and cut into pieces to be fed to a shredding machine. About books stacked in lorries and driven away into the unknown.

One evening Jesse brought me a section of a book which had drawn her attention because of its special paper and type. It was in Latvian but looked nothing like the thin, grey-paper products of our publishing houses.

'A section of a book is also a book,' said Jesse, proud of her find.

I flipped through the pages aimlessly. Then I chanced upon a dialogue which sent shivers down my spine.

'Do you believe in God, Winston?'
    'No.'
    'Then what is it, this principle that will defeat us?'
    'I don't know. The spirit of Man.'

Who was this Winston who was asked about God just as I'd been asked on Engels Street before going to Leningrad?

I read on. The whole dialogue sounded as if the speaker was standing right beside me, in my narrow room, as if he was describing my life right now.

*

We could have had a lovely last summer together, if Jesse had not brought us that portion of book. My mother devoured it, and Jesse and I counted the days until the ambulatory centre would reopen. Jesse regretted her find from the bottom of her heart. We even debated taking the book away from my mother, but the consequences would have been unpredictable. In the beautiful light summer evenings in the garden my mother talked only about her 'book of revelation', which Jesse had rescued from the archives.

I began to go out in the evenings, leaving my mother with Jesse. Jesse sat faithfully beside her in the garden and listened to endless tirades about Winston, this new stranger who had completely overshadowed Ishmael.

With frequent turning and consultation, the pages of this half-book began to disintegrate. Looking for sturdier paper, my mother eventually took our calendar and wrapped the book in that. The inscription on it in red said 'Novij 1984 god' – 'New Year 1984'. She crossed this out and wrote in black ballpoint: 'Summer 1984.'

I hated this half-book wrapped in a calendar. It had stolen my last summer with my mother and led her even further into a fantasy world, away from life, the blooming garden and the balmy river.

*

I floated through my daughter's departure as if wrapped in mist. My daily reality had blended with Jesse's book. My life no longer felt as though it was mine. July and half of August sped by at savage speed. Eventually Jesse took the book away and hid it somewhere. She could no longer look on as I ruined my last few days with my daughter. I admired my daughter. She didn't show her disappointment and patiently tolerated my odd absence, while carefully packing the things she would be taking to Riga. She had found a part-time job at the post office, to earn some pocket money, and in the evenings she wasn't home, but she never came back later than midnight. Maybe she was in love? There was no time for her to tell me about it. Jesse found this the most painful thing. The day she took the book from me, she said that I was behaving like her mother, who had left her on the orphanage steps with the note: 'I don't want this gift.'

'Are you even aware,' Jesse said, 'that she'll never be with you in the way she is now? She'll move on into her own life. She's an intelligent and good-natured girl – she's a blessing. What are these devils tormenting you?' Jesse spoke as if delivering a sermon.

My devils – my *besi* – I had tried to talk about them with Serafima, but she hadn't believed me. Or refused to believe me. But Jesse saw them in me.

'Mamma, I'm not going to take my old school uniform. I'll leave it in the wardrobe.'

We were sewing a new uniform – a skirt, a checked blouse and a blazer – and my daughter was busy chasing away my *besi*.

'I won't take my school bag either; it's worn out inside. Nor the ski boots; they pinch my feet. And, if it's OK, I'll leave the fairy-tale books. I won't have time to read them now. The dog's collar I'll put in the lower drawer of the wardrobe. Maybe you'll get another dog. And don't forget to water my Christmas cactus now and then. And, please, don't overwater the tiny green plant with snakeskin star flowers. Mamma, what do you think: should I get a fringe cut? Maybe I should have a bob? You know, I'll leave my neckerchief. There's no sense in taking it along. All right? And here are some other bits and pieces – stones, chestnuts, the herbarium. They won't be in your way, will they?'

'No, they won't be in my way, my child. I'll be fine with them in my cage. I'll pick them up every couple of days, blow off the dust, air the room, water the flowers. Slavery is freedom, child. I'll be right here, waiting for you.'

Slavery is freedom. I learned that from my book.

The night before my daughter left we sat for a long time in the garden. The August night was humid and warm. Then my daughter asked, 'Mamma, does any child remember how her mother's milk tasted?'

'I think they can't. You can't have memories that early.'

We sat on in silence.

*

I returned to Riga and my grandparents. In the whirl of beginning at my new secondary school, for a while I forgot about my mother. Even though I had my own spacious room, I often slept on the pull-out chair in my grandmother and step-grandfather's room. We wanted to be together as much as we could manage.

The new school was tough. It was enormous. Some of the classes took place in the old building, some in the new. The two buildings were joined by a long glass corridor and riddled with smaller and larger labyrinths of corridors, along which one had to get around every day. There were only a few newcomers in the class. Classmates kept their distance from each other just as the teachers kept their distance from the students. The headmistress sat alone in her office. Approaching her was strictly prohibited. Everything was quite the opposite of my experience at our small country school. In those first weeks of September I almost missed the rainy beetroot and carrot fields, the early mornings when we used to sit all together by the heaps of green stalks and leaves, and warm soup was brought to us there in the fields.

Everything here was different. Sterile, clean, cruelly lit by the bright ceiling lights. Everyone in this city school was competing to be the best. And the head, a vast woman with grey hair and the shadow of a moustache, encouraged all of this. When she appeared in the corridors, everyone froze. Even the gym teacher, who at least matched her in physical volume.

The romance of the beetroot fields was exchanged for twice-weekly school cleaning. On cleaning days, classes ended earlier. We had to scrub the floors and radiators, to make up for what the cleaners missed.

When the work was done, the headmistress would emerge. She wore a large white glove on her right hand for inspecting the areas we had cleaned. Of course, grey and sometimes even black smudges would appear on the white glove, to be followed by a lecture in the great hall. All Soviet students bore responsibility for honestly done work. All young communists' consciences must be as white as her glove – before it acquired the stains of someone's shoddy work.

During these lectures in the stuffy, low-ceilinged auditorium, my conscience started to ache for Bambi. I suddenly understood the poor hamster. Mentally, I begged his forgiveness. What's more, as I waited to be liberated from the stifling hall and the head's penetrating voice, I remembered how my mother had sympathized with Bambi and eaten the mushrooms, not knowing if they were safe or deadly.

I began to question my grandmother and step-grandfather about their life. Were things always like they were now and how the announcers told us it was on TV every evening?

My step-grandfather said one shouldn't dwell on the past. Nothing would change here. The Russian boot would be here for ever. And, for God's sake, he added, above all, I must not to talk about any of this in school. Even with those I considered my friends.

But I was not to be stopped. I told my grandparents about the time my mother got drunk after Brezhnev's funeral, about the red-white-red Michaelmas daisies on her table and about all she had said about Latvia.

My grandparents stared at me in horror, then they both started to cry. My step-grandfather brought a photograph album from the stack in my room.

'This autumn you'll be a big girl,' he said, 'but you must understand that this has to stay in our house. Because nothing, absolutely nothing will change here.'

'You have to live with how things are, Sweet Pea,' my grandmother added.

But my step-grandfather's album was like a fairy tale. A tale of Latvia before I was born and even before my mother was born. My step-grandfather was in it, wearing a beautiful official uniform, in knee-high boots and holding a flag at the Freedom Monument. The sepia-toned image muddled the colours. 'Two red stripes and one white,' my step-grandfather said. 'We had our own state and our own flag.'

Now tears also filled my eyes, because my mother had said the same thing. All of this had seemed to me no more than her own dark nightmares, but now it turned out to be the truth.

What to do with the truth? The school timetable included six Russian language and literature classes every week. And we had to study the Communist Party Congress documents, which repeated the same meaningless phrases again and again. All of these empty phrases had to be memorized, then recited.

My life divided into parallel worlds. After school I worked hard on my homework for the next day, but in the evenings I listened to my grandparents' stories. They knew so much.

Up to the first autumn break I got excellent marks in the new school. My average mark in school was exceeded only by our school's wunderkind. A mathematician and an honours student, no one could compete with him. I admired his quick mind. Indeed, I came to trust him so completely that I wanted to share my parallel-world stories with him. I wanted to talk about our Latvia being mocked by the Soviet Union and Germany, about refugees, about executions and deportations to Siberia, about the ones who remained and were silenced, as we, the third generation, were already silenced. I wanted to talk about my mother, who lived in a desolate place in the country because she could not live two lives – and could not accept a life of mockery, as Latvia had been mocked. I wanted to share all this but I didn't. I obeyed my step-grandfather, who knew what he was talking about.

During the autumn break I went to my mother's. Jesse met me at the railway station. Her face showed distinct signs of anxiety. I hadn't seen my mother for almost three months.

'It's a vale of tears,' Jesse said as she walked beside me. 'She now goes to the ambulatory centre only a couple of times a week. The rest of the time she is slowly self-destructing. I try as hard as I can, but nothing works. I clean the house, but she doesn't let me into her room. It's good that you've come.'

My mother was lying in bed in a heavy bathrobe. Scattered around were books, ashtrays, half-eaten apples. The small bedside table was loaded with coffee mugs, and half-empty pillboxes lay littered beneath it.

She smiled slightly when I entered.

'So you've come, city girl,' she said as she lit a cigarette.

The air in the room was stale. I opened the window.

'Mamma, look what I've brought. Pears, a persimmon and edible chestnuts. Do you remember? The Central Market is full of them, and they're not so expensive now.'

My mother touched the yellow pears and the flame-coloured persimmon.

'They're probably very fragrant,' she said. 'But I can't smell them.' She inhaled apathetically.

'I'll stay with you for the whole week. Get up,' I said. 'We have to clean this room.'

My mother submitted like a child. She sat in the kitchen while I tidied her room. In the evening I heated a large tub of water. I helped her to wash and scrubbed her back. I brushed her tangled hair and cut her toe- and fingernails.

'I do pull myself together a couple of times a week. I have so little strength. I don't want anything,' she said. 'Jesse tidies this and that.'

'Tomorrow or the day after tomorrow, could you bake an apple cake?' I diverted my mother's thoughts. 'We have to celebrate our birthdays.'

During the days that I was at my mother's, she livened up somewhat. She listened with interest about my new school, about our evening stories, about the wunderkind with whom I wanted to share some stories but refrained.

'Mamma,' I said, 'I didn't believe what you said. Now I know, you were right about Latvia.'

'You're a smart girl,' my mother said.

We invited Jesse to our birthday celebration and to share our apple cake. She came in her best clothes, her hair prettily curled.

At our festive table Jesse took out a small box. It was the only gift she had been given by her foster mother in the orphanage. She wanted to give it to us.

'Open the box,' Jesse said to me.

I opened it. Inside was a gold ring, a bit of candle wax and a dried twig.

'Jesse, aren't you sorry to give it away? It was a gift to you, after all,' I said.

'It was freely given. I freely give it away,' Jesse said, laughing.

We sat late into the night, talking nonsense. I looked on as my mother returned to life. Jesse was happy here with us.

*

'Now it will be like this for ever. She'll come during school holidays, sometimes on weekends. Sometimes, when she's busy at school, she won't come. When she falls in love, she'll come even more rarely. This is how it will be now, Jesse.'

'You've been in bed for three days in a row. Get dressed. Let's go for a walk.' Jesse never lost hope that I'll be able to crawl out of my hole.

'Cigarettes and books have torn you away from real life. Those damned pills too,' Jesse mumbled, gathering mugs and ashtrays.

'They make it easier for me, Jesse,' I said. 'If only for a moment, I'm in another world.'

'What's wrong with this world?' Jesse asked. 'Tell me what's wrong with it? In the mornings the sun dawns, in the evenings it sets. The days pass peacefully. We don't have serious ailments, we're not starving. We have our homes.'

'Jesse, when you talk like that, I almost start to believe you.'

'Admit it, admit this truth,' Jesse continued. 'Then you'll be free for once.'

'But Jesse, I've never been a slave to them – the cigarettes, the books and the pills.'

'Truthfully you're not?'

'I'm not, Jesse. This is why I feel free.'

A little offended, Jesse left my room. I heard the clattering of dishes as she washed them in the kitchen.

I forced myself to get dressed and we went out for a walk. It was a tranquil November, the kind that stirs an ache for the past. We walked in silence along the river in the direction of the *kolkhoz* fields. Beyond them lay the meadows. Hardly anyone went there any longer, maybe only in the summers to gather herbs for tea and wild flowers. But Jesse and I liked it here. The meadows led back to the overgrown riverbank, where bulrushes browned and shimmered, touched by the first frost.

'Look,' said Jesse, 'they've not turned to fluff, they've just frozen.'

'Jesse, what shall I do? My soul is sorrowful enough to die. It's frozen,' I said, looking on as she touched the bulrushes.

Jesse was silent. The river was silent in front of our very eyes. The overcast sky was silent.

We walked back home along the path by the river. Jesse walked in front. I followed in her footsteps. Suddenly she stopped and turned around.

'For God's sake, pull yourself together,' Jesse said.

Jesse then started telling me about the orphanage, where boys had tied her to a post, a rough post thick with splinters. They had tied her almost naked, in her skimpy undershirt. They made her say, 'Better that I hadn't been born!' Jesse had stayed silent; as if her mouth was full of water, she'd stayed silent. But they had yelled, 'Say it, you freak, say, "Better that I hadn't been born."' But Jesse had kept silent, as if she had a mouthful of water. Then the boys had thrown stones at her. They'd hit her legs, her face, her arms. And they had continued to yell, 'Say it, say it: "Better I hadn't been born."' But she had suffered and in silence. Not once in her life had she said those words. Then she had lost consciousness.

When Jesse finished speaking, she turned and went on her way. I continued to walk in Jesse's footsteps.

*

Returning to Riga after spending the autumn school holiday with my mother, I was still uneasy about her. It was a comfort knowing that Jesse was with her. Not wanting to worry my grandparents, I told them that everything was more or less fine, that my mother was now working less and resting more, something she deserved to do long ago. I said we had had a wonderful time, that we had baked an apple cake, celebrated our birthdays, roasted potatoes on coals in the wood stove, and that I had breathed good country air and the days had flown by.

I was now into my second term at school. I could not let my marks slip after finishing the first term so well. The wunderkind had begun to pay attention to me, which was a great honour. We had a heavy course load. Military training had been added to the curriculum. We all had to lie on our stomachs on the school's smelly gym mats and spread our legs wide (which amused the boys no end, for the girls were not allowed to change into trousers), then aim a rifle at a target and pull the trigger when the instructor yelled 'Shoot!' Anyone who couldn't follow his orders received the instructor's favourite line: '*Po druzhbe dvoyechku*' – 'For friendship's sake, do it twice.'

His cruelty paralysed us all. He was quick to dole out 2s – the lowest grade on your report card – which could ruin a high grade average. After the shooting exercise we had to don gas masks, removable only at the instructor's order. One friend fainted because it turned out that her mask's valve was closed. She nearly suffocated while waiting for the order.

I hated that short, fat instructor. In my imagination he became the culprit for this Soviet absurdity of parallel lives. Then a ray of light pierced my hopelessness. A call for applications to a cultural history group appeared on the school bulletin board. The meetings would take place outside class time. Of course I applied.

Three students came to the group's first meeting: myself, the wunderkind and one other girl. We were introduced to Teacher Blūms, who looked as if he came from another world. He had a high forehead, bushy, longish hair and a thick beard. He didn't even look like a teacher. He spoke in a quiet voice and what he spoke about was quite otherworldly.

We were to begin with poetry. At these meetings we were to learn what our school curriculum had missed out. Our first text was a poem titled '*Krasta runa*' – 'The Seashore Speaks' – written by a poet only ten years older than us. Teacher Blūms recited – and we three sat transfixed. Just a moment ago, we had been gasping for air in our gas masks, waiting for our orders. Now we were standing on the seashore, where waves rose and broke.

With Teacher Blūms, my new parallel world bur-
geoned at lightning speed. In the Gorky Street library
I found the poet's first published book. The slimmest
of slim volumes, already the worse for wear. I shoved it
into my boot and strode out of the library. And I read it
from the first poem to the last and back again from the
last to the first.

*

The director at the ambulatory centre now seemed to
look at me with suspicion. Several times she commented
on my slipshod appearance, which, according to her,
didn't do credit to a doctor who was seeing patients.
My workload was reduced to a minimum, but during
consultation hours the corridor was packed to overflowing. Therefore, at least for the time being, the director
tolerated my presence.

I had once more fallen under the spell of Winston.
Jesse had taken great pains to hide the half-book, but I
found it nonetheless. Winston followed me everywhere.
Like a shadow that walked ahead of me whenever sun-
light fell on my back, as if mocking each step I took. He
accompanied me to and from the ambulatory centre. He
stood behind me in the consulting room and, shamelessly,
didn't even turn away when my patients undressed. In
the evenings, I often saw him slithering by outside my
window. In my dream he had become the man from my
grandmother's story, the one who slept in a ditch, covered

with a church windowpane. He protected his face, protected it from a view of the future, where a boot trampled the face of humanity. He had been warned to do so. Now Winston firmly told me to do the same.

Poor Jesse tried hard to pull me away from his spell. On my days off she appeared early. She encouraged me to go into the garden or for walks. She forced me to get involved in making our lunches. She bought a live carp from a neighbour. The carp king himself: he was enormous, with a moustache. He was so beautiful that we decided to lengthen his life. We slid him into a tin tub full of rainwater. I sat by the tub and looked on as the big fish circled. Jesse warned me not to grow attached, for his end would come no matter what. But I sat and occasionally churned the water, so that the king would have enough oxygen to breathe. Gratefully he opened and shut his mouth and flashed his golden mirrored sides in the tub.

'But Jesse, how can we kill him? Look at his beauty,' I said.

'With a big knife.' Jesse said. 'You'll hold him, while I will smack him on the head with the knife handle and then slit him at the gills. We'll roast him in the wood stove on the coals.'

'Jesse, you're not listening to me. What a beauty, how can we kill him?'

'Better come and hold this: he will make several suppers,' Jesse persisted, tying an apron around her waist and arming herself with a big knife.

It wasn't easy. The king resisted and evaded us like the devil himself. He slapped us with his tail, he jumped into the air. It was a difficult battle. But Jesse's big hands were powerful. The head was off – but the king was still moving. The mirrored scales flew to all sides under Jesse's sharp knife.

Our evening meal was delicious. The king melted in our mouths.

'I'm telling you,' Jesse said, 'I'll go fishing myself. There are a lot of fish in the river.'

'I'll go with you,' I said to Jesse gratefully. At least for the moment, Winston's shadow had disappeared.

*

Attendance at our cultural history group increased with every meeting. Already we were twelve. Each Wednesday meeting with Teacher Blūms introduced something new. So all week we had a new poem or painting, a historical building or symbol to think about. This was so exciting that my interest in the ever more senseless subjects taught at school diminished markedly. For example, in social studies we had to recite our new state leader Comrade Gorbachev's first speech, which he began by extending his sympathy for the death of his predecessor, Comrade Chernenko, who had for a short while replaced the rapidly deceased Comrade Brezhnev's successor, Comrade Andropov. We had to learn by heart that:

the Communist party of the USSR is by its very nature already an international party. Our confederates abroad can be assured: Lenin's party in the struggle for peace and social progress, as always, will collaborate closely with the brotherly Communist, worker and revolutionary democratic parties, will stand for the solidarity between all the revolutionary powers and for active cooperation. In order to resolve the complex tasks that have been presented to us, we have to further strengthen the party, increase its organizational and leadership role. The USSR will always be based on and continues to be based on Lenin's idea that principled policies are the only right policies.

My head threatened to burst. What we had learned from the comrade's speech was slowly eroded by what Teacher Blūms was reading to us: 'Whoever takes hold of the realm and wants to manipulate it will have no peace. The realm is a sacred vessel that should not be interfered with.'

I started to hate my school subjects. I needed my head for the other, more meaningful things being planted there by Teacher Blūms.

One Wednesday he asked all of us to meet at the bus station the following Saturday, bringing knapsacks with sandwiches and tea. Our group was to make an excursion. I had already planned to go to my mother's house, but Teacher Blūms' invitation was enticing. After all, as it was the winter holiday, I'd still have time to visit my mother.

That Saturday morning, after several hours, the bus halted at a remote country stop. Outside it had iced over, although there was still no snow. Following our teacher in single file, we crossed an untended field to reach an old church. The door was half-open. The teacher closed it temporarily. We stood outside the church. He told us about the people who had built and cherished it, who had come here to pray, to christen their children, to hold weddings and funerals. About the bell-ringer, who had gone deaf from the ringing, about the minister, whom the bell-ringer had betrayed, and about the altar painting that had disappeared.

Having concluded its story, he opened the door to the church. Inside were ruins, on which bushes and saplings had sprouted. Through the broken windows we could see a bleak sky. A mute church bell hung above us.

We all looked up.

'See,' our teacher said, 'the bell had its tongue torn out. It can no longer ring.'

Later, by a campfire near the church, over sandwiches and tea, the teacher asked us what thoughts the bell had inspired.

As always, the wunderkind had to be different. He said that the bell had been lucky in a way, because it never had to worry about holding its tongue again.

Everyone, including Teacher Blūms, laughed heartily.

'And what do you say?' the teacher asked me.

Everyone gazed at me in silence. The fire was crackling. The flames and the silence burned my cheeks.

'That bell reminds me of my mother.'

The silence and the crackling grew louder.

*

My daughter came during the winter holiday. For Christmas Jesse had set up a spruce branch with large cones in her room. She had dusted and washed the floors.

In the kitchen Jesse's cooked peas were drying in their pot. Jesse had wanted to make it a beautiful Christmas, but I had shown no interest. She was probably offended. She had left our clean, tidy house and the holiday treats she herself had prepared. She had not returned for the holy days, not even for New Year's Eve.

My daughter was busy in the kitchen. For the first time in days the enticing smell of food invited me to get up and dress.

'I doubt Jesse will come again,' I said from my room. 'You too will soon stop coming.'

'Mamma,' my daughter called back from the kitchen, 'now, you can't give up just like that. I'm stewing ribs with sauerkraut. Before the New Year your stepfather queued at the butcher's for hours, and we bought the sauerkraut in the market. They send their best wishes to you, and also a little gift.'

Stewed ribs and sauerkraut. A gift. The small things in life. I felt a pang of pain at the thought.

With great effort I put on warm trousers and a jacket.

I had already hurt Jesse, my good, faithful friend. I didn't want to hurt my daughter too.

She was quietly humming in the kitchen. Just as Jesse did, she was breathing life into it. The pot was simmering away. Warmth emanated from the wood stove. The coal and the ribs in the sauerkraut wafted their aroma.

'Mamma, the coals are ready. Let's put in potatoes in their skins. Do you have potatoes?'

'Potatoes? Maybe. If Jesse brought them, maybe we have some.'

My daughter exclaimed happily, 'Look! Here are some in the pail in the pantry. I'll wash them.'

I sat down at the kitchen table, lit a cigarette and gazed at my daughter's movements. They were womanly and domestic, joyful and considered. How she raised the pot's lid and tasted the contents, how she added salt, how she scrubbed the potatoes and lined them up on a neatly folded towel to dry. How she organized the dishes, knives and forks on the table, how she put butter in the small dish, and the candle and spruce branch in a tiny vase.

We sat at this festive table in this island of our lives. She talked enthusiastically about her school, about the wunderkind and Teacher Blūms, who was the cleverest person in the world.

'Mamma,' she said, 'do you remember how you made me up to be two people – a split personality – for our school carnival? Now I really am a split personality. One half is taught at school, the other is taught by Teacher Blūms.'

Suddenly she became embarrassed. She asked, 'Mamma, will you be offended if I tell you something?'

'I won't be offended.'

'Teacher Blūms took us to an abandoned church, where we saw a bell that had lost its clapper. Afterwards he asked what we thought about the bell.'

'What did you answer?'

'I said that the bell reminded me of you. Everyone was silent and I didn't have anything more to say. It was quite a dreadful silence, but I couldn't explain briefly why that bell reminded me of you. That's why I kept silent.'

'And why did the bell remind you of me?'

'Because it often seems to me that someone has stolen your joy in life. They've torn it out of you like that bell's clapper. And you can't ring any more – just like the bell. Are you offended?'

I gazed at her. My flesh and blood. Her longing for life was stronger than the evil that gnawed on me.

'You're not offended?'

'No, of course not. You're my joy.'

After the meal we dressed warmly and went outside. It had snowed for three days. The bright sun covered the white earth with its veil. We headed for the river down our accustomed path.

'Along the way let's stop by Jesse's,' my daughter said. 'Jesse is a good person and no one should hurt her.'

My daughter threw a snowball at a window of Jesse's modest house. After a moment she came out, warmly wrapped and happy to see us.

'Jesse, what a lovely day!' my daughter called out brightly. 'Let's go to the river.'

We went as a threesome. My daughter walked in the middle, her arms around the two of us.

The golden ball of the sun rolled out over the white river. We stood dumbstruck, moved by the radiant silence.

Then my daughter exclaimed, 'Let's slide on the ice! Mamma, Jesse, let's slide!'

She grabbed our hands and we raced for the river. We slid back and forth until we collapsed in the soft snow. For a moment all three of us lay there, holding hands. Gazing at the sun.

*

After the winter holidays at my mother's, I continued to attend Teacher Blūms' group and to distance myself from the school curriculum. This began to bring down my high marks. My form teacher was concerned. I promised to pull myself together. My grandparents were also worried. Had I too much to do – with the school and the cultural history group as well? No, I insisted, everything was fine. Privately I fretted about one thing: that my form teacher and my family might start to look askance at Teacher Blūms. I forced myself to master the school curriculum. I learned all that foolish history and social studies, wrote required compositions, became a model of obedience in military studies, somehow scraped through in chemistry, physics and algebra

– and my grades began to improve once more. All this in aid of a single objective: Teacher Blūms had promised to take us to Leningrad and to the Hermitage during the spring holiday. If I received a good report, no one would object to the trip. Grandmother sighed, because she remembered how badly Leningrad had turned out for my mother.

'Please stop,' I said to her. 'Don't ruin the trip I'm so excited about.'

The trip was a good excuse for not visiting my mother during the spring holiday. I wrote to her explaining that a wonderful trip was on the cards for me – to Leningrad. She sent me a postcard with a view of the River Neva and its bridges, surely from her time in Leningrad. On it were only two sentences: 'Have a wonderful trip. My greetings to Neva and Teacher Blūms.'

I could hardly believe it, but it did happen. On the second day of our spring holiday, we were sitting in a second-class carriage on the Riga–Leningrad train. I had studied until I was sick to my stomach and Teacher Blūms had kept his word.

The next morning, having hardly slept, we headed straight for the Hermitage. We stood at the end of an impossibly long line, ready to draw on all our reserves of patience, for it was very cold. Beside us, a stream of foreigners flowed rapidly into the building. They had arrived in comfortable buses and were welcomed inside without spending any time out in the cold. As we queued and froze, we took turns to leave the line to hop and run about a bit. It was well past lunchtime when we got into the Hermitage.

After the first two exhibition halls my head started to spin. I found a bench and sat down. Here was a world to sweep you off your feet. I didn't attempt to understand Teacher Blūms' descriptions. I just allowed his words and the paintings to flow through me like fine grains through a sieve, catching here and there, and sprouting in the fertile soil of my imagination.

Time stood still. We wandered through the halls as if possessed. Soon we were close to exhausted. Then I saw a brilliant green moon set in a black painting. I sat on the floor before the painting and could not leave. The painting drew me into its darkness and its light, which were fighting each other in the small, square-framed space. I was there between the green moon and the darkness into which everything vanished – me, my mother, my grandmother and step-grandfather, the hamster in its cage, the tiny clay figure I had made. Everything spiralled as if in a whirlpool, then vanished into darkness.

I came to my senses. Teacher Blūms was saying, 'You fainted by the Kuindzhi.' The frightened members of my group stood around me. The museum guards had brought a glass of water.

At night we went to see how the bridges are raised over the Neva. The bridge jaws gaped open and rose majestically to meet the star-filled heavens. Below flowed the river that I was to say hello to from my mother.

*

My daughter came to see me four weeks after her spring holiday. She had grown thin. She spent her time in her room or in the kitchen gazing apathetically out of the window. Something had happened.

We weren't accustomed to questioning one another. In the evening muffled sobs issued from my daughter's room. I stepped inside.

'Mamma,' she said through tears, 'after the Leningrad trip they let Teacher Blūms go. Someone told the headmistress that I fainted by a painting and he was let go. But that's not all.'

'You fainted by a painting?' I asked.

'Yes, I was tired and I had my period. Besides, that painting was incredibly beautiful, just the darkness and a green moon. I looked at it for a long time. Then suddenly it was as if the darkness drew all of us into it – me, you, Grandmother and Step-Grandfather, and the little clay baby. It grew dark in front of my eyes and I fainted.'

She cried so dreadfully, weighed down by a great guilt that should not have been hers to carry.

'That's no reason to dismiss a teacher.'

'It was only an excuse, Mamma. It turns out they had been watching our teacher from the very first day our group met. It turns out that someone among us reported everything, absolutely everything, to the headmistress. She relayed everything on to the KGB.'

I sat by my daughter's bed, listening. A wave of suffocating hatred washed over me. It was as if the ghost of Winston was standing outside the window. The marks of his torture were visible – he was hardly recognizable. He had been forced to confess and to accept 'their' truth. This spectre that had burdened me for so long now also burdened my daughter.

'But that's not all, Mamma,' she said, through tears. 'A week after the trip, the head called me out of class and led me to a room beside her office. It was like that time when we had graffiti scrawled on the pavement. There, in that room, sat a dreadful man. Dreadful, Mamma, with a massive head, light hair and evil eyes.'

I stroked my daughter's head. Shudders passed through me as if rushing in from a distance – from the stand of young spruce trees which my father had tried to protect, from the cold suitcase in which my mother had hidden me, from the old professor who had reported our talk about God, from the Engels Street room in which I denied everything, from Serafima's husband's ugly face, from my Soviet cage, where I went on living without the courage to eat my child. I fought with all my strength against this battering. My hands must not tremble. I must comfort my crying child.

'He asked me, "Did Teacher Blūms take you to a church?" straight out like that. I was so frightened by his evil expression that I just trembled and said nothing. Then he walked behind me, Mamma, he placed a hand on my shoulder and said in a chilling voice, "You won't graduate from this school, and you'll never be accepted at a university if you don't answer." And, Mamma, I said he took us! I said he took us, Mamma,' my daughter sobbed. 'I should have lied, said that he didn't take us, but I told him the truth, that he took us.

'The evil man went on tormenting me. "Did he read poetry and other texts to you that aren't in the school curriculum?" I said he did read them, and I was crying. I should have lied and said he didn't, but I told him the truth, that he did read them. Mamma, I should have denied everything and lied. And then he returned to his desk, pulled out a blank sheet of paper and a ballpoint pen and placed them both in front of me. And in just as cold and calm a voice he said, "And now you'll write all this down. You'll write that Teacher Blūms took you to a church and read poetry and other texts that aren't in the school curriculum to you. And you'll sign – your name, surname and class."

'I refused to write. The evil man got up from his desk once more, Mamma. He stood behind me once more, but this time he put both hands on my shoulders and squeezed them so hard it hurt.

'"You do know, of course, how life has turned out for your mother" – that's what he said, Mamma. "By tomorrow you'll be expelled from school, and your good marks won't help you."

'He turned me around to face him. His face grew red and he was yelling.

'"Comrade Blūms' sort poisons our young, poisons and leads them away from the Soviet path. If I had my say, he would be in prison. Unfortunately, these are no longer the times for that. But he will not set foot in this school again. Never again. Write!"'

How my child wept then. I tried to comfort her.

'And then, Mamma, the door opened and the head-mistress came in. Her face was hard and mean. She sat down at the desk, crossed her thick fingers and started talking just like that evil man.

'"Now you have the opportunity to ruin the rest of your life. The others have already written their pieces and signed."

'"All the eleven others?" I asked through tears.

'"All eleven and without such melodrama," she replied.

'Mamma, that means the wunderkind had already written his confession! And then the head added, "If you didn't have such good marks, I wouldn't go so easy on you. Write and sign it." And then, Mamma, I did write it.'

My daughter was crying so dreadfully that my heart was breaking.

'I wrote that Teacher Blūms took us to a church and read poetry and other texts that aren't in the school curriculum. I wrote and I signed my name, surname and class.'

I brewed some camomile tea with honey for my daughter. She drank it and fell asleep, having wept until her tears ran out. When I heard her breathing calmly, I closed her bedroom door.

The darkness in my room enveloped me. I opened the window. Outside, spring was in the air. I lit a cigarette. The shudders slowly receded.

The sky was unusually bright. I stepped into the garden. Such a star-filled sky! Directly above my head flowed the Milky Way, unreachable and infinite. I gazed at it all night until dawn. I gazed until the Milky Way vanished and a cockerel began to crow in a neighbour's yard.

*

Without Teacher Blūms, school felt empty. I tried not to catch the wunderkind's eye – although he behaved as if nothing special had happened. I avoided meeting the rest of the group, but when I ran into them accidentally in the school corridors, they also behaved as if nothing had happened. Everyone had spring on their minds. Just a little over a month and the summer holidays would begin. I had caused so much worry for my grandparents. After the interrogation, they worried about me so much that it became a burden. They had decided to rent a couple of rooms by the sea and spend the summer there. I decided to go to my mother's.

I managed my schoolwork as if on automatic pilot. I learned all that I was assigned. My form teacher was keeping an eye on me. In history and social studies classes I was forced to work much harder than my classmates. I submitted, and spent all my time studying. I counted the days left until the end of the school year. I had a calendar in which I crossed off every day that passed.

It was already the end of April when the country was shaken by the explosion of the Chernobyl power station. The school director tripled our military instruction classes. On the instructor's orders we put on and took off gas masks until we were sick and tired of it.

My form teacher told us about the doctors and volunteers from Latvia who now had to go and help in Chernobyl. As an example she mentioned her son, who was a doctor. Her duty as a mother was to convince her son that his place was in Chernobyl. She had succeeded in doing so. Now her son had gone to the nuclear disaster site to help the victims.

I didn't understand this teacher's dedication. Encouraged by her, her son had put himself in harm's way. But I didn't have to understand anything. I had only to heed what constituted duty to our great motherland, and to have the courage characteristic of a responsible Soviet citizen.

I gazed out of the window and the teacher's words passed me by. On the other side of the street, the tall chestnut trees had burst into leaf. Soon the trees would be in blossom. I would leave the city, run through fields, swim, sit for hours on the riverbank, encourage my mother to go for walks, and we wouldn't go to bed until late in the warm evenings. I would drag my mother out of her lair littered with books, ashtrays, apple cores and coffee mugs, and we'd pick the first chanterelles in the woods. I would read all that Teacher Blūms had recommended. I'd read all that was on my mother's bookshelves. I would read to spite the man with the evil eyes, to spite the headmistress and my other eleven classmates who had denounced Teacher Blūms, to spite myself for denouncing him too because I was intimidated. I hated my fear. The summer seemed like a liberation from what felt like a young offenders' institution. I only had two more years of it to endure.

'I am proud of my son.' The teacher's words called me back to the class.

Two weeks later, when the chestnut trees were almost in blossom, tragic news ran through our school. Our form teacher's son, the doctor, had been killed in Chernobyl. She walked around dressed in black with a black ribbon tied in her hair. Everyone expressed their sympathy to her. She had to wait for a zinc coffin to bring her son back from his duty abroad, which she had encouraged him to fulfil.

In her sorrow she became even harsher. Although it was almost the end of the year, she harangued us with new history to learn, adding more and more homework and tests.

While we were doing the tests, she would disappear into her office. Her muffled sobs could be heard through the wall. We hunched over our notebooks so that we wouldn't have to look at each other. Towards the end of the hour, having dried her eyes, she would come back into the classroom. She would bark, 'I am proud of my son. He fulfilled his duty.'

I saw how a cage had materialized around her, how she had shrunk and mutated into a hamster devouring its child. It was so real and horrifying an image that I felt sick. There was a numb silence in the classroom.

The summer didn't bring the liberation I had antici-pated. The day before I was to leave, Jesse appeared at our front door in a state of near collapse. She stammered, 'Your mother is alive. They transferred her to the big new hospital right here in the suburbs.'

'Jesse, what happened?'

We sat her in the kitchen and made her drink my grandmother's tea. Soon she was able to tell us what had happened.

After my last visit, my mother had withdrawn com-pletely. She hadn't even gone to the ambulatory centre for the paltry two days a week she was still meant to work. 'I really don't know,' Jesse said, 'but I think she was let go from her work.' When it got dark, she had sat outside, gazing at the sky. Jesse had tried to talk to her without success. All she got was broken phrases, answers for the sake of answering.

Jesse had tried to cheer her up: 'Summer's coming, and all three of us will be here together. Everything will be OK.' My mother had turned to Jesse, looked at her in a funny way and said, 'Yes Jesse, yes. Everything will be OK. We are all only human.' And my mother had gazed upwards again, into the darkness.

On the evening of that day, Jesse had come by after work to make dinner. The door to my mother's room had been closed. Jesse had knocked, but my mother didn't answer. Jesse had sensed that something was terribly amiss. She had knocked more persistently, but still nothing. The door was locked simply with a small latch. Jesse had managed to get it open.

'My God,' Jesse said. 'She was lying there with her eyes open, her pupils dilated, her hands groping at the air around her. Scattered beside her lay two packets of pills – she had swallowed the contents of both.'

My grandmother bent her head. 'The road to hell,' she repeated, 'the road to hell.'

Jesse continued. She was allowed to go along with my mother, who had nearly died in the ambulance on the way to the hospital. Her stomach had been pumped out. Now she was still in intensive care but her condition had stabilized. Jesse was not allowed to see her, but they would let in a daughter or her mother.

Jesse talked for about twenty minutes. But to me it felt like twenty years of talking, and those years went by right here in our kitchen, where outside the dandelions were already blooming in the yard and soon the lilacs would join them. My grandparents would sit beneath those lilacs, happy once more to feel the first spring warmth. And toddlers might play in a sandpit at their feet, and the birds would take sand baths. But I had no time for that spring. I had to grow up fast, faster than the words flowing from Jesse's mouth. And I had to be brave to hear out her story.

'Jesse, stay the night with us. Take a bath, rest,' I said.

'Yes,' my grandmother agreed weakly. 'Jesse, stay with us.'

'I will try to go and see her tonight. First I must phone the hospital.'

'Sweet Pea, you won't go alone, will you?' my grandmother asked.

'I will go, and I must go alone.'

At the end of Lenin Street, the tram turned off towards a pine forest. It was half-empty. I sat at a window. Everything my grandmother had given me to take along lay in my lap: a toothbrush, toothpaste, slippers, a dressing gown, a hairbrush, soap, underwear, warm socks. Beyond the window, in the woods, bushes were sporting their first spring green – so bright they dazzled me. Near the hospital some old ladies were selling spring flowers.

It was the busiest visiting hour. People were hurrying over the stone slabs of the hospital entrance hall, to bring their loved ones home-cooked food, flowers and life's necessities.

The doctor on duty in intensive care listened to me attentively. He set my passport next to my mother's.

'You're very young,' he said. 'Are you sure you want to see her now?'

'Yes,' I answered.

I followed the doctor down never-ending corridors. It felt as if we were descending deeper and deeper into the underworld. At last the sign 'Intensive Care' appeared in blue lights.

'She's not conscious. Poisoning one's system with pills is life-threatening,' the doctor said as he opened the door to the ward.

My mother lay in bed naked to her waist. Adhesive patches stuck to her chest were connected to tubes which in turn led to various pieces of medical equipment. On a nearby monitor the line of her heartbeat zigzagged.

I smoothed my mother's hair. It was matted as always. I stroked her ear, her neck and chest. She was warm. Warm and quiet, she slept, transmitting her life signal to the metal box.

After a while, the doctor came in.

'I think we'll pull her through,' he said. 'You too must help to call her back.'

Three days later, my mother regained consciousness. She was transferred to the regular ward. My grandmother and I sat on either side of her, while my step-grandfather waited outside on a bench so that my mother would not get too emotional during this first encounter. She ate a couple of spoonfuls of our broth, closed her eyes, and said just these few words: 'It's a pity.'

My grandmother had a long talk with the doctor. Their decision had been made. They were ready to transfer my mother to the psychiatric hospital, where she would have to stay for at least a month under medical supervision. She would have to be medicated.

'We have no choice,' he explained. 'She tried to take her life. Consciously tried, despite being a mother and a doctor.'

The summer passed me by. Both by the sea with my grandparents and in my mother's house with Jesse, all we thought and talked about was her. I went to see her at the psychiatric hospital three times a week. I had to sign in. The hospital orderly would attach a doorknob to the door and let my mother out for a walk with me in the madhouse yard.

We walked in circles or sat on the broken benches. Mother smoked greedily and constantly, as if I had brought her the elixir of life in cigarette packets.

'Say hello to Jesse,' she said. 'And Mother and Stepfather.' She repeated the same thing again and again. I could not muster the courage to ask the question that was tearing me in half.

'How is the sea?' she asked. 'Do you also go over to our house? Jesse must be taking good care of it.'

She asked and I answered with a brief yes or no, for sure, good, as always.

'You don't want to talk to me,' she concluded, suddenly offended.

'You don't want to live,' I threw back.

'I don't want to,' Mother responded.

'So what will happen now?' I asked.

'They'll sign me out after a month, after determining what category of disability support I fall into. Then I'll return home. I want to be at home. It's dreadful here. Inside.'

'And we, Mamma, will we have to live in constant fear for you? I'm afraid for you. I'm afraid, Mamma. I've been afraid since my early childhood.'

'Forgive me, I'll try. I'll try! Forgive me,' my mother repeated, in fits and starts, as she smoked.

'Look, Mamma, everything is in blossom around us. We could sit in our garden, chat with Jesse, whip up a strawberry mousse, walk in the fields, swim in the river…'

'Hug me. Hug me tightly and kiss me,' my mother said. Suddenly her face was revealed to me in the sharp light of the sun. It had aged all at once. The smooth skin hung loose, dark hollows lay under her eyes, and deep lines of sorrow stretched away from them, as if etched into her hard face by the constant flow of salty tears.

I hugged my mother and kissed her.

'You've returned. I called you back so fervently, you've returned. Everything will be fine, Mamma.'

*

They eventually signed me out towards the end of August. The female doctor in charge treated me as if I were the lowest creature on earth. A mother, a doctor – but a Tvaika Street psychiatric patient. They filled me with enough medication to fell a horse. I allowed them to.

My daughter and Jesse came to help me pack and to take me home. They tried to talk about all sorts of trivia until we were standing outside the asylum gate.

'Listen! Never again will you have to be here,' Jesse said with determination.

My daughter held tight to my hand. She led me as if I were an unruly goat who might slip away from her at any moment.

'I stole your summer,' I said to her.

'There are still a couple of weeks left. We'll be able to go mushrooming,' she replied matter-of-factly.

My clean, orderly home and garden welcomed me. What pains the two of them had taken! My room smelled of apples. There was a vase of Michaelmas daisies on the table, which had been laid for a meal. Life was waiting for my return.

They busied themselves around me, warmed up food, unpacked our bags. I looked on. I wanted to stop what was happening as one stops a car in order to hitch a lift. But all that was happening passed me by. I wanted to say, 'Jesse – stop fussing! We're on the Milky Way, playing, dipping our legs in until our feet disappear.' But I was silent. I looked on as they organized me to go on living.

'I've managed to get work for you,' Jesse said happily. 'Tying wire brushes. To clean off rust. You can make good money. There's no need for any documentation; the work will be formally in my name.'

'Tying wire brushes?' My daughter was not convinced. 'But Jesse, maybe Mamma can still go and talk about a job at the ambulatory centre?'

'Nothing will come of it there,' Jesse said. 'Word has reached them. They know everything that happened.'

'Tying brushes, Jesse – that's magnificent, thank you. I'll tie wires with all my heart and soul.' I said it genuinely, but my daughter and Jesse heard irony in my voice.

'Can you get something better? How much disability compensation will you get and when?' Wounded feelings could be heard in Jesse's words. 'I'll help you in the beginning. I know how. It's not complicated work,' she continued.

'Fine, Jesse, fine. We'll tie brushes.'

I felt weak and went to lie down in my room. My daughter covered me with a blanket.

'Sleep for a while, Mamma. Rest,' she said, stroking my head.

Half-asleep, half-awake, I heard my daughter talking with Jesse.

'She's given up completely. She's smarter than all of us, more courageous than all of us. She's an excellent doctor, Jesse, she knows about saving lives. But, Jesse, she also knows how to die. How can we support her? Why should she submit to this injustice? She was supposed to work at the Leningrad Institute! But now you're going to teach her to tie wire brushes! What is this life in which I have to betray Teacher Blūms and my mother doesn't want to live at all?'

'Don't talk like that,' I heard Jesse say, trying to comfort my daughter. 'This is the hand that we've been dealt. We're worn out from carrying heavy burdens. Everything has to be accepted with humility, even wire brushes. Then you'll regain your strength of soul.'

'Jesse,' said my daughter, 'you speak beautifully, as if you were a book.'

I dozed off. Sleep set me free. Then they woke me for dinner.

*

The new school year soon came round. My form teacher took particular care of me. She continued to wear a black ribbon in her hair. Several times she asked how my mother was. I answered politely that everything was fine. One day she called me into her cramped cubbyhole of an office.

'You can't let things slide in any subject. Your marks have to be exemplary.'

'I am trying.'

'I know where your mother was this summer. And then there's the Blūms case. You have to be exemplary so that no one can accuse you of anything.'

My harsh form teacher's face suddenly thawed. She clasped my hand and began to speak quite differently.

'Dear child, you have to keep your chin up. You can't slip up in any way. You have to be the best.'

Dear child? I was stunned.

'I'm often afraid for you,' she continued. 'Afraid you might fall apart. All your troubling experiences with your mother.'

I suddenly felt sorry for her. 'Teacher, everything will be fine. My mother is better, and she has someone who looks after her.'

'Good. That's very good,' she said, and offered me a sweet. 'But all this must stay between us two, agreed?'

'Agreed, Teacher.'

My marks improved. My combined autumn and winter school report was very good. For both the school holidays I forced myself to go to stay with my mother. She had settled, to a degree. Jesse supplied the brush bases and the wires, and my mother had become adept at tying them, demonstrating as much talent in this as she had in consultations with her patients. In fact she was earning just as much. For each of the school breaks she supplied me royally with pocket money – fifty roubles.

I brought gifts for my grandmother and step-grandfather back with me from each of those visits. Sometimes my mother baked a cream of wheat cake, other times I brought home a roast chicken, and other times she made stuffed cabbage. Everything she made tasted good.

In the middle of January, the headmistress called us all into the large auditorium. We were to listen to a lecture read by the wunderkind. His topic was the first issue of a new literary journal. Along with the head, the wunderkind ridiculed and slandered the journal from the first page to the last. 'Is this poetry?' the head almost yelled. '"One should not climb on a toilet, for then big, black footprints are left on a white cistern." Is that poetry?' She asked and answered her own question, and glared at the assembled students in the hall. All this public derision of the journal only increased our interest in it. The first issue was passed from hand to hand and read from cover to cover. Teacher Blūms would certainly have recommended it as obligatory reading.

But in February something ghastly happened. In the seaside resort of Jūrmala a young poet was pushed out of a window in a tall apartment block. He was the poet whose poem we had read for our first workshop:

The sea rises and crashes, rises and breaks apart again
(Others rise and crash, rise and break apart again.)

He gazed out at me from the obituary in the paper with
curly, longish hair, square-framed glasses and a manly
face. How could he be dead?

I discovered the date and location of his funeral. I
told the girl who shared my desk at school that I would
go to the funeral, even if it was during class time. She
was a great gossip and soon all the class knew of my
intention. More and more people applied to go. Now
we were almost the entire class, except for the few who
were afraid.

On the day of the funeral we attended the first two
classes. Then we gathered in the cloakroom to get ready
for the trip. Our form teacher and the headmistress
caught us on the school steps. Someone had informed
them, of course.

'You won't be going anywhere,' the head said, her
face white with anger. Our form teacher stood beside
her wringing her hands.

My classmates kept looking at me.

'We're going,' I said to the head. 'All of us are going.'

I suddenly felt the same power I had that time in
primary school when the sweaty man was challenging
me about my mother.

'We are going,' I repeated, while a feeling of nausea
rose inside me, for I remembered how the head and the
KGB man had forced me to incriminate Teacher Blūms.

'We are going,' I said again as clearly as I could. 'And then you can expel us all.'

Our group started on our way. The head and my form teacher remained outside on the steps on that freezing February morning.

We pooled our money and brought some flowers. By the time we reached the graveyard, they were frozen. And there was a sea of people there. We mingled with the crowd, never again to be separated from it.

*

Jesse was a real master with the wire. Patiently she taught me this new trade. In the beginning my hands were hurt, but slowly I became more skilful. It was mechanical yet, in its own way, creative work too. The wires had to be drawn with a special bent needle through the holes of a wooden base and then nipped off in equal lengths. Jesse wondered at my dexterity. 'Well, you used to sew up women's flesh.' And she fell silent, thinking perhaps that I could be offended by this mention of past times. But those doors were closed. The wire brushes formed a large pile. At the end of the week Jesse brought boxes into which she carefully packed the brushes. She was paid in cash for them. She continued to clean at the ambulatory centre. She also continued to tell me about the patients there who wanted consultations and kept asking when I would return. She thought she was keeping my spirits up.

As I drew each wire through the base of the brush, a calm space grew in my head. It was something like sleeping, only with open eyes and hands in movement, repeating their gestures over and over. The work steadied me. It also prepared me for something that was irretrievably closing in. As Jesse had said in that half-whisper to my daughter: everything must be accepted with humility, even wire brushes. Then we can regain our strength of soul.

I had almost given up reading. Neither Ishmael nor Winston haunted me any longer. I now saw them as poor lost souls belonging inextricably to this world – a world I would have to leave behind sooner or later. And there was no way they could help me at that point of departure.

I tried to put aside the very best for my daughter. Two days before her arrival Jesse had gone to the nearby town to hunt for groceries. She had her ways and her favoured places. Green peas, peppery sausage, occasionally oranges or squid – all under-the-counter wonders, not to be found on store shelves. As a brush assembler I could afford much more than I'd been able to on my monthly wage at the ambulatory clinic.

When she came for her spring holiday, my daughter told me about the poet's funeral. And how afterwards at school and in the atmosphere generally something had changed.

'Mamma,' she said, 'something is near at hand. Everyone can sense it, but no one is talking aloud about it yet.'

I listened to her enthusiastic voice and kept quiet about my premonitions.

Jesse had an urge to mock my daughter's enthusiasm. Waving a dishcloth over her head, she exclaimed, 'Freedom or death!' then fell silent, glancing at me with guilty eyes.

'Jesse, don't treat her like a brainless child,' I said. 'And, really,' I added, 'all of us are the living dead here.'

Silently Jesse handed dishes to my daughter, who dried them. On the table the old clock went on ticking.

*

The last year of secondary school sped by. Before the exams my form teacher once more called me into her cubbyhole office.

'You've studied so hard that you've earned it.'

'Earned what?' I asked.

'We could excuse you from the final exams.'

I was struck dumb by this offer.

'Why, Teacher?'

'It's a lot of pressure and, taking into account your mother's problems, one never knows how your nerves will react.'

I felt as if she had doused me with cold water. Maybe she intended it for the best, but this pity degraded me lower than the floor we stood on.

'Thank you, Teacher, but I would be happy to sit my exams. You don't need to worry about me.'

'Think hard about it,' my form teacher said. And, leading me out of her cubbyhole, 'Remember such a possibility exists.'

That day I didn't go home after my classes. I went to the small park where my grandparents often used to take me when I was younger. It still had the same broken benches, potholed paths, overgrown flowerbeds, littered sandpits and old swings. It was a spring afternoon. The only people there were an old couple sitting in the sun. I put my schoolbag down beside the sandpit and sat on the swing. I pushed off with my feet and began to swing myself higher and higher. A tingling began in my stomach. I swung higher still. My mother wasn't pushing me on the swing. She had never taken me to the swings; I had no such childhood memory. I was swinging on my own. I tried not to touch the ground with my feet, not to brake this free-flowing movement. The warm spring wind in my hair. A cloudless sky above my head. I embraced the gifts of living and breathing.

After a long walk I came home late. My grandparents tried not to show their anxiety, although I saw it in their eyes. They had got used to my routine – school, home, homework, school, rare visits to see my mother.

After supper and homework, sleep came quickly. But sleep brought a dream I had had before. I'm clinging to my mother's breast and trying to suck on it. The breast is large, full of milk, but I can't get any out. I don't see my mother, she doesn't help me, and I'm left to struggle with her breast on my own. Suddenly I succeed and a liquid flows into my mouth. But this time it's not bitter – it's as sweet as camomile tea with honey. I suck and drink and drink to my heart's content from my mother's soft, warm breast.

*

'Mamma, I was accepted! I was accepted, Mamma!' She almost tripped over the pile of wire brushes as she stormed into the house. Breathlessly, she told me about her strange summer of studying behind heavy curtains, so that the sun wouldn't tempt her to go outside. She described the national competition through which girls from country schools who had *kolkhoz* and Soviet farm recommendations and who only got grade 3s out of 5 in all their subjects might still be accepted at university. She described the old professor who had saved her life in the literature exam: she had been unlucky, drawing a topic to defend on contemporary life difficulties in the novel *Zīda tīklā* – 'The Silk Net'.

Jesse and I had waited so long for her. The summer had felt endlessly hot. Working at those wire brush piles, despite my skill, I always had fine scratches on my hands, which became inflamed in the heat. My fitful, dream-filled sleep reminded me of the summer when I was expecting my daughter. Memories of blurry visions: of a light that shines into me as I stand at the window, that gathers behind my breastbone and pierces painlessly through me to emerge from my head. However much I wanted to, I couldn't turn my head to see if it was all the same light. Intrusive thoughts about children as the fruit of sin assailed me. I contemplated bastard children brought up by wild-animal mothers or left in baskets at rich people's doorsteps or set afloat in rivers. I considered maidservants made pregnant by their masters, who jumped into rivers or died at the hands of quack doctors. I dwelt on women abortionists of the offspring of sin, who had gone mad, been driven away or burned on pyres.

Here she was: my daughter. Not a bastard, nor the fruit of sin. Thirsting for life, she lay in our garden, where Jesse's multicoloured autumn blooms and her yellow dill flowers spread their fragrance.

'Mamma, come and lie down beside me,' she said. 'The sun is still so gentle and the grass is warm.'

I went out into the garden and lay down beside her. She took my hand.

'You've got lots of scratches from those brushes, Mamma. You have to go back to the ambulatory centre, at least try to. Do you know what happened in the city's streets this summer? Your stepfather said it was unbelievable. It looks as though everything is about to change and we will be set free. Maybe you can even try returning to the city. You're a brilliant doctor after all. You'll find work for sure.'

I clasped my daughter's hand tightly and said, 'Yes, freedom is close at hand, I feel it. It's no longer far away.'

'I never know when you are speaking from the heart and when you are speaking just for the sake of saying something,' my daughter said.

'I throw the dice for words from the heart. Let them fall as they may.'

Jesse was calling us to lunch. She set out tiny new potatoes with a wild chanterelle sauce and freshly salted pickles.

'Maybe you'd like milk with this,' Jesse suggested. 'We have some here, from a neighbour's cow, milked fresh yesterday.'

'No,' my daughter replied immediately. 'Jesse, definitely no milk for me.'

'Do you still get nauseous from milk?' I asked.

'I don't know, but better not to try it,' my daughter said, cutting me short.

For a while we ate in silence. Then Jesse suddenly began to tell the story of a loner who had gone off into the hills because he was disappointed in people and the world they had created. She talked breathlessly as if she'd waited a long time for an audience. Where did she get these stories? From the discarded newspapers, or the torn and shredded books?

Forgetting the delicious meal, she went on: 'He took with him only his cane, which was more faithful even than a dog. The cane helped the loner to climb the steepest hills, cross the most dangerous passages, traverse the longest of roads, which led him away from the world that had chosen the wrong path. The loner didn't have the power to lead so big an entity as the world onto the right path. That's why he left: at least he need not be a factor in others' choices. Leaning on his cane, he had gone sufficiently far to feel his absence from the world. Amid hills under a wide blue sky, he had air to breathe freely and an unpoliced road under his feet. But this first impression, as so often, turned out to be deceptive, for pretty soon the loner started to grumble – first to himself, then at his cane. Thus he spent several years, until he suddenly realized that, having left the world while leaning on his cane, he still had no right to call himself a loner. When he came to a bridge over a fast-flowing river, the loner threw his trusty cane into the current. That wasn't easy; for many years they had walked hand in hand. Now it seemed to the loner that he had freed himself from his last earthly burdens. Yet, no matter how far he went, more and more often the loner felt that he was dragging along all the world's burdens. And now he had to carry them alone, for he no longer had a cane…'

Jesse fell silent. The potatoes and mushroom sauce on her plate were getting cold.

'Jesse, you have such great stories!' my daughter said.

I was sitting in the kitchen at the table, Jesse on one side, telling the story while her meal got cold, my daughter on the other side. Everything slid past me: Jesse's story, the garden beyond the window, the warmth of my daughter's arm as she brushed against me taking away the dishes. Everything slid by.

*

That autumn, when I started my first university course, we were still sent to a distant Soviet *kolkhoz* to help with the harvest. Even there a sense of change hung in the air. Everyone – the administrative staff as well as the common workers – drank from morning till night. We were squeezed into a couple of multistorey buildings that stood in the centre of the region. From there we were taken to do hell's work. The rotted grain had to be shovelled together with the good grain, probably to increase the overall volume. The same with the potatoes, which were gathered by a terrible old harvester machine. It held boxes where we had to pile stones and then the potatoes on top. In the midst of all this the drunken Soviet *kolkhoz* director kept shouting, 'May this whole kit and caboodle go to hell!'

The month dragged on until it felt like a year. We had to survive this interim station where they had managed to strand us once again. I spent the evenings in bed with a small flashlight and *Zarathustra*. He asked pointed questions of me, to which for the moment I had no answers. My hands still reeked of rotten grain. Before my eyes flashed the potato harvester, while the stones in the potato boxes rattled on into my sleep.

One day in the drying-kiln I accidentally waded into some bilge. My legs were drenched to the knees. No one was able to drive me back to our barracks that day. After returning with the others and spending a sleepless night, by morning I had a high temperature. My university colleagues covered me with their blankets, left me the tea kettle and went out to the fields. I remained on my own.

I slept in a feverish semi-consciousness. My broken sleep brought strange visions. I was knocking at the door of our building in Riga. Oddly it was locked. People leaned from the windows – but they had all died. There was Mrs Migla, whose baby had died on the train to Siberia. His little body had been rolled down the railway embankment between stations. And Mrs Frišs, who used to tell how she had been saved from the Nazi executioners in Siberia, and Mrs Mežinskiene, who didn't talk about anything. And there, high up, was my mother leaning out of the attic ventilation window. She had something clenched in her fist. She let go. A large key landed at my feet. The windows closed one by one and everyone disappeared, including my mother. I picked up the key, cleaned the sand off it and tried to unlock the door. But the key got stuck and I couldn't turn it either way. I very much wanted to get into our flat, where my grandparents were probably having their supper. My mother might even be there too since she had thrown me the key. But the door would not give. I awoke in a sweat, bundled in blankets in the clammy room.

My illness took some time to subside. I was allowed to go home. There, cared for by my grandmother and step-grandfather, I gradually got back on my feet, although I was often ill again during that first year of university. The days passed monotonously. Only my mountains of books could transport me into a different life. Jesse visited now and then, with greetings and gifts from my mother.

I managed to get good marks in the spring term, although I suffered the consequences. I would read until I felt sick. Often while immersed in a book, I would suddenly feel nauseous and have to run to the toilet. Like my childhood reaction to milk, it wasn't because I didn't like something about *The Odyssey* or *The Brothers Karamazov*, but because the words made my head spin.

Now the first year was behind me. Once again summer was beginning and I was going to stay with my mother. We hadn't seen each other at all during my long winter of illness and reading.

She had come to meet me at the train station. She stood by the flowerbed, strange and distant. It was like that time she had come to meet me at school and we didn't know how to behave. We hugged. My mother's hands were covered in gashes, which she had become used to. I tried to look at her face, which I had last seen in that nightmarish sleep, when she threw our door key down from the attic window.

We walked in silence, as usual.

Surrounded by the signs of early summer, the road led my mother and me towards a new life. It promised that everything would truly turn out well. Indeed, our road was beautiful. White and blue anemones greeted us from the edges of ditches. The sky was clear. Somewhere in the distance a cuckoo made its bubbling sounds. The birches still showed that bright, bare greenness that dazzles one's eyes. My mother's cigarette smoke mingled with the spring air and heralded something unknown, something fresh and appealing. It drove away the sadness of separation and comforted my aching soul.

It really was a wondrous summer. Laughing and joking around, the three of us tied the wire brushes at speed. We wanted to amass sufficient money to spend on all kinds of small things. 'Like manna from heaven,' Jesse exclaimed, when we returned with treasures for the soul and the flesh.

Late one evening in midsummer I talked my mother into coming for a swim in the river. There was no one on the bank, so we could swim naked. My mother undressed covertly, as if she was shy. But once in the water she said, 'Warm as milk.' For a while we floated there together. The moonlight threw a bright path across the water. My mother swam into it and I swam beside her. We swam until we were nearly out of strength, then turned back to the bank.

*

She left at the end of August. That autumn was particularly rainy and dank. We had to keep the wood stoves burning constantly so that our hands wouldn't freeze as we tied the wire brushes. From the world outside Jesse brought alarming news. Everything was truly about to change. Freedom was close at hand. On those evenings she talked like a prophet.

'Maybe the time has come to put the wire brushes behind us?'

'Jesse, do you think there's room to be found for freedom here?' I answered with a counter-question.

Jesse looked at me as if I were a hopeless case and exclaimed, 'How long are we going to sit on the fence?'

That night I couldn't get Jesse's words out of my head. Unable to fall asleep, visions came to me of a long road with crowds of cripples moving slowly along it. Tottering, they dragged themselves forward, driven by some tantalizing dream. Yet they were after all limping towards life. I wasn't on that road. I didn't see myself there. The road came to a fork – one branch led the cripples along an earthly road and the other was the milky way to heaven. There will be plenty of room there, Jesse. There will be space for freedom. Life will have healed over and our lives will be released into the wide world.

Time was moving more quickly. Sometimes I sat in my room for days on end, smoking and staring, as morning became midday, midday became evening, and evening became night. Jesse noticed that I was switching off. She decided to come to live with me. On my active days, we would eat a late breakfast, tie a batch of brushes, then prepare for lunch. Towards evening, Jesse would go to clean at the ambulatory centre. I would try to read something, but the letters slid past my eyes and nothing stuck, nothing stayed with me.

When Jesse returned, we would talk about my daughter. We were waiting for her. This second year felt harder than the first. She had to study and read so much that she had less and less time outside her course even to come and see us. Jesse spoke up to ask if I wouldn't like to see my mother and stepfather. We could pull ourselves together, crawl out of our wire-brush den and go to the city. But I had no such desire. Sometimes I actually felt my strength draining away. Nothing hurt, I had no fever, just an odd condition of weightlessness.

Often I couldn't sleep at night. Jesse guarded my sleeping pills like a prison officer and dispensed them as parsimoniously as communion wafers. They were my redeemer and my joy. That tiny white pill – one and a half or two – which transported me away from the cripples' earthly road even if only for a moment.

My daughter came at Christmas. Only for a few days, but she came. She brought gifts – my mother had knitted a hat for me and mittens for Jesse. My stepfather had made a pair of candle holders with his own hands. My daughter gave Jesse and me each a crocheted angel, bought on a street corner from an old woman who also had an angelic air about her.

My daughter herself was the greatest Christmas gift for Jesse and me. She had grown more beautiful, more serious and more adult. Possibly she was in love, but she wouldn't talk about it. Instead she talked about books and theories and begged to borrow *Moby-Dick* from me, as well as the book about Winston, which Jesse had hidden along with the sleeping pills.

She told me about my mother, who was spoiling her, and about my stepfather, who had experienced sudden heart palpitations, but they had called an ambulance in time and everything was fine once more.

After our supper, she went to her room. Jesse had made up a bed for her and lit the wood stove. It was already midnight when she came into my room. She sat on my bed. As usual, we spent a while in silence.

Eventually she said, 'Mamma, do you remember how you drew a mother and a baby – that picture with the two of them dancing around happily joined by an umbilical cord?'

'Maybe,' I said.

'I have a strange feeling that that is not how it is with us. For us the cord is cut – yet it seems you still hold me with it. We are still connected by a sort of transparent but very strong cord, and I sway along with you, everywhere you sway.'

She didn't wait for my answer but pulled up my blanket, kissed me, wished me a good night and left the room.

*

I didn't go to my mother's again until the spring. Jesse came to the city a couple of times. She didn't hide that she was worried about my mother. More and more my mother would sit for hours in her room gazing out of the window at a single point. The ceiling of her room had yellowed with the cigarette smoke. Jesse's tone conveyed unspoken reproach at my not coming to visit more often.

'But do come this summer, this summer for sure,' she repeated. 'That will be a prompt for her to pull herself together and to connect to life again.'

It seemed to me that since I was born I'd been trying to get my mother to connect to life. As a helpless infant, as a child of limited understanding, as a fearful teenager, as a young woman. And she always seemed to be striving to turn out her life's light. So we struggled – always ending in stalemate. Although one day the light would be extinguished for ever.

Out in the streets, the summer of 1989 was on fire. The people out there were transformed: elated and happy, armed with flowers, folk songs and little red-white-red flags. Life flooded the gardens, courtyards, roads, fields and cities. I wished that like the ninth wave it would crash through my mother's small, smoke-filled room, wash away all of history's injustices and miserable coincidences, including being born exactly then and there – crash in and let life in with it.

But my mother didn't leave her room. She didn't leave even when Jesse and I, crying with happiness and helplessness, told her that she had to join hands with people throughout our three Baltic countries who wished to be free. We would form a living human chain in which every person had their place. Every one of us would become part of that causeway of human beings, extending our hands to each other, and no one would be able to destroy us again.

But my mother wouldn't come out. Jesse and I stood hand in hand with many others and cried not for joy at the freedom which was close by but because of our heartache for my mother, who refused it.

I left earlier than planned for the city. I knew that I was leaving the entire burden on Jesse's shoulders. With every passing train station I distanced myself from my mother's stifling room, where she gazed at the August garden through the half-open window or maybe simply stared at a point in the distance and saw nothing.

In the lecture halls September passed as if we were in a trance. No one talked about literature or historical Balt grammar. Everyone – lecturers and students – behaved as if set free from imprisonment. The only thing that mattered was what was happening outside. The mighty Soviet monolith was tottering, collapsing, and no one could tell if the consequences would be the devastation of an earthquake or as it was in the Bible when God created a new, beautiful world out of nothing. Would it be a paradise or hell?

One sunny October afternoon, we lived and breathed nothing but the People's Front Congress. The people demanded the return of their mother – the land of their birth. My grandmother and step-grandfather didn't hide their tears of joy.

In the evening Jesse telephoned. She couldn't talk. Tears stifled every word. My mother had died. I had to hurry back immediately.

I arrived on the last train. Jesse met me at the station. She had shrunk into a tiny creature, her face ridged with pain and tears. We walked along the leaf-strewn road. The beginning of October was oddly warm.

'I don't know. I don't know what she did to herself,' Jesse sobbed. 'I came back from the ambulatory clinic and she was lying there – dead. A doctor came and certified her death.' Jesse cried like a child.

I walked beside her, not yet understanding. The news of my mother's death seemed unreal, invented. Even though weeping Jesse testified to its truth by every sound she made.

With our neighbours' help, Jesse had carried my mother into the garage. She lay on the long table in her old housecoat and woollen socks, her hair in a ponytail. Very likely she hadn't brushed it.

I touched my mother's hand. It was cold and covered with gashes from the wire brushes. I took her hand and tried to warm it in mine, but it made no difference.

'Heat up some water, Jesse,' I said. 'Let's wash her.'

In the mixed dimness of electric lamps and candle-light I unbuttoned my mother's housecoat. Jesse helped me to undress her. It seemed to us that my mother must feel cold, so we covered her to her waist. Jesse brought warm water, alcohol and towels. I wet the towels and first carefully cleaned my mother's face. In the corners of her eyes she still had remnants of sleep, and a crumb of bread in a corner of her mouth. Her lips were dry and chapped. Then I carefully washed her breasts – which I had only seen once during a night swim, when we had slid into the river naked. They were cold, white, with a scattering of tiny freckles. I touched them. They rose from my dream warm and full of mother's milk, and the milk flowed life-giving and infinite. I rested my head on my mother's breasts, and my warm and salty tears fell upon my mother's cold flesh.

The next morning I returned to Riga. There was much to do before the funeral. My grandmother and step-grandfather divided the tasks. We worked together, trying not to show our emotions. Jesse remained with my mother and cried for all of us.

The unusually warm October air flowed through the open window into the kitchen, where we were eating our supper in silence. I gazed at my grandmother's pale cheeks and at my step-grandfather, who had bent over his plate so we wouldn't see the tears falling into his food.

Tomorrow we would have to bid farewell to my mother. When the table had been cleared, my grandmother asked me to stay a little in the kitchen. After a moment she returned with a small bundle wrapped in white cloth, mottled with rust stains. She untied it.

On the kitchen table under the wan lamplight, my grandmother unwrapped the tiny parcel. It was a baby's first shirt and bundled within it was a horseshoe with a couple of nails. So that the infant would be lucky in life. It belonged to my mother, once the tiniest of tiny infants. And the horseshoe was a lucky one that my grandmother had found for her on the war-ravaged road, so that her life might be peaceful.

It was a strange funeral. Without anyone to lead my mother into the next world in accordance with the ancient Latvian custom, the funeral took place in silence. The October sun and its golden leaves strewed the paths. There were four of us at the graveside: my grandmother, my step-grandfather, Jesse and I. An endless stream of women unknown to us flowed by, leaning down and placing flowers on the grave mound. A blanket of deep red, then white, then deep red Michaelmas daisies.

Jesse and I lit candles. May my mother rest in peace. Several women embraced me, without a word. But a young woman of about my age came up to me and spoke in Russian.

'My mother, Serafima, called your mother my father.' She smiled. 'Without your mother, I would not have been born. That was in Leningrad. Now we live here. Serafima died, but she always said that I should find your mother. Sadly, I have only managed now.'

'Your mother was my father' – it rang in my ears.

In the evening I lingered in my mother's room. Jesse had brought in autumn flowers. Everything had been cleaned and put in order, but on the table stood my mother's ashtray with the last cigarette butt and a half-drunk mug of coffee. I looked up at the ceiling, where Jesse had done her best. She had scrubbed at the dark-yellow smoke stains and managed to clean away almost all but a tiny circle in the centre.

I lay down on my mother's bed. My mother's fragrance was there – and not there. Maybe Jesse had changed the bedding. Under the pillow I felt something hard, wrapped in paper. As I unwrapped it, into my lap fell a tiny clay baby. Suddenly I remembered it word for word, as if in black and white, a simple story of which even the tiniest fact could not be verified because no proof of it existed except in my memory. I had wanted to recreate a foetus out of clay.

On the paper my mother had scrawled:

Thou, who hast given birth to the Healer, heal my soul of yearning and sinful passions. Tossed in life's storms, lead me to the port of penitence. Save me from eternal fire, the evil worm and hell.

About a month after my mother's funeral, Jesse came to our flat in the city. She had continued to live in my mother's house, tending the garden and at first walking to the graveyard almost every day.

After our bathtub ritual, about which Jesse used only one word – heavenly – we prepared for supper. My grand-mother had made a special effort: a roast with vegetables, a cream of wheat mousse for dessert. We were setting the table when, from the other room, where the television was turned on, my step-grandfather shouted.

'This can't be true! Quick, quick – come here!'

Scared, we ran to him. On the television thousands of people were shown climbing onto the Berlin Wall and tearing it down bit by bit. There, on the screen, reigned an uncontrolled joy, euphoria, the sound of yelling and streaming tears.

'This can't be! It can't be!' As if transfixed by the screen, my step-grandfather repeated it over and over.

And yet it happened right in front of our eyes. Our four pairs of eyes – mine, my grandmother's, my step-grandfather's and Jesse's. Only my mother's were missing.

Jesse clutched her head and said, 'We really will be free. Why couldn't she listen to my words?'

Subscribe

Discover the best of contemporary European literature: subscribe to Peirene Press and receive a world-class novella from us three times a year, direct to your door. The books are sent out six weeks before they are available in bookshops and online.

Your subscription will allow us to plan ahead with confidence and help us to continue to introduce English readers to the joy of new foreign literature for many years to come.

> *'A class act.'* GUARDIAN

> *'Two-hour books to be devoured in a single sitting: literary cinema for those fatigued by film.'*
> TIMES LITERARY SUPPLEMENT

A one year subscription costs £35 (3 books, free p&p for UK)

Please sign up via our online shop at www.peirenepress.com/shop

reference
in Bible
15 October 1969
Daughter/Granddaughter
22 October 1944
Mother/daughter

the writer is
the daughter/
granddaughter
NO
Two voices

G but they're
not on
speaking
terms!!

2 1st person narrators { daughter/mother
{ daughter/granddaughter

Peirene is proud to support Basmeh & Zeitooneh.

Basmeh & Zeitooneh (The Smile & The Olive) is
a Lebanese-registered NGO. It was established in
2012 in response to the Syrian refugee crisis.
B&Z aims to create opportunities for refugees to
move beyond being victims of conflict and help
them to become empowered individuals who one
day will return to their own country to rebuild
their society. Today the organization is managing
nine community centres in the region: seven in
Lebanon and two in Turkey.

Peirene will donate 50p from the sale of this book
to the charity. Thank you for buying this book.

www.basmeh-zeitooneh.org

Look of the
Golgotha
p. 152
Mother's litany

green mary
painting

p. 150